Happy Birthday
Mari H !
Best Magical
hope you en

May 22

Edited
by
Ginger Fyre Press & Bekki Milner

GINGER FYRE PRESS UK
Typesetting © Ginger Fyre Press
March 2022
Ginger Fyre Press is an imprint of
Veneficia Publications

Misty Morgan

Witch of Elphame

C. J. Delahay

Contents

Contents

Introduction

Outside the window, a strong gale blows,
The glass rattles in its frame.
Whistling wind seeps through the gaps
Calling out her name.

The rusty lamp flickers, the light goes dim,
There's a shadow on the windowsill.
A waft of sweetness kisses her nose
As she lies shivering in the chill.

Beyond the window the moon is full,
It shines with a silver glow.
Its shimmering light smiles down
On bleak streets and concrete below.

From the darkened hallway
The clock ticks away time,
The pendulum swinging
Awaiting the chime.

Tick ... tick ... tick ... tick
The clock beats with her heart,
"Misty!" She hears her name,
"It's now the time to start" ...

CHAPTER 1

To guess the exact time would be impossible, or so she thought. She could hear the rhythmic sound of the old grandfather clock tick tock-ing in the hall, echoing in her ears. It was much louder now, as during the daytime she never noticed it at all.

"I guess, hmm, ten minutes to ten," she said to herself, biting her lip, hoping this time she would be right.

She rose from the creaky pull-out bed in the living room and tiptoed out to the hallway, being careful not to cause any noise that could disturb her father Robert in the next room.

"Yes!" She shrieked loudly. For the first time in her twelve years, she saw the second arrow touch the golden number ten, meeting the already present arrow on the same sparkly number. She jumped on the spot whilst stretching both arms into the air in jubilation. The feeling of accomplishment lasted approximately thirty seconds, if that, as she heard the roaring voice of her father and heavy footsteps heading toward the door.

"Misty?" Her heart sank as she crept quietly back to her makeshift space, which in fairness was only a metre or two away but seemed like a mile.

"What are you doing? Get back to bed, NOW!" Her father's voice almost knocked her off her delicate but grubby feet and her heart sank with each booming beat.

She scuttled into the living room, flung herself onto her bed and grabbed the thin duvet, yanking it over her entire body with just the top of her head and a few ginger wisps of hair poking out, and pretended to be asleep. She waited for the vibration of the footsteps, then the bed shook as the door to the living room flung open. She squeezed her eyes shut, tensed her whole body, and waited.

"What have I told you?" Said her father angrily. Her eyes were still shut but she knew he was stood at the foot of the bed. "Sit up and look at me, NOW!"

She did what she was told. Staring down at her with bleary eyes, beer bottle in his left hand and his right, clenched in a tight fist, stood her father. The lecture that followed was just noise to her, feelings of anger boiled in her chest, and she could almost feel her heart pop right through her night shirt. But to keep the peace and avoid any further argument, she promised she would go straight to sleep and not disturb him again.

The door slammed shut and again she was alone. The murmuring sounds of conversation in the room next to hers was distracting, she knew he was on the phone to someone and wondered for a moment if it was

Mum. So, she put her ear against the wall and listened intently. His voice was low and sounded serious. She heard him mention her name, then her brother Michael, then silence but for the clinking of another beer being opened. She sighed and laid back down on the bed. She hadn't seen Mum or Michael for five years and the memories of them were fading as fast as the hope of ever seeing them again. All she had left were a few old photos and some boxes of Mum's things in the basement. She rarely, if ever, went down there. She told herself it was better that she forgot them, but that didn't mean that she didn't dream about them. But to dream she had to sleep, and so it was better to stay awake.

Misty lay there thinking about the clock in the hall, the only reminder of the cottage in the countryside that she'd shared with Mum, Dad and Michael, her happy place. The place she called home. Dad had lugged that clock around with them with each move they'd made since leaving there five years ago, and there'd been many moves, each one as bad as the last.

What was that? She thought, a sudden noise jolted her from her memories. There seemed to be something moving outside her window. She sat up and although the curtains were drawn they were thin, and she could just about make out the shadow of something outside on the ledge. She thought it looked like a cat, at least she hoped it was, otherwise what was it? Then she heard a little meow and a tap-tap-tap on the glass. She considered her options for a moment, staying in bed safe from harm or discovering the mystery beyond the curtain and potentially getting another ear bashing. Her inquisitive mind won over and before she could talk herself out of it, she was out of bed and peeling back the curtains.

The cat on the windowsill looked at her. Their eyes met and she had the strangest feeling that she had seen this cat before. But where? When? She could not recall, yet the cat did seem very familiar.

"Hello puss" she whispered softly, careful not to alert her father again. "How did you get here? Silly fatty puss." She felt warm inside, her fears evaporating into the night sky. The cat stared at her but without moving his mouth he spoke, she heard the words, clear as day.

"Hello Misty."

Her eyes were wide now, her heart felt like it had stopped beating and she froze on the spot.

"I'm Shadow," the cat said, the glass that separated them now glistening in the moonlight.

"Pleased to meet you Shadow," she replied. She did not know why she responded that way, the words just fell out of her mouth. What she really wanted to say was *How come you can talk and how did you get on my window ledge when it's six floors up*?!

"I have something for you Misty," said the cat, and with a mischievous smile he was gone. A cool breeze followed, which caused goose bumps on her arms, the back of her neck prickled, and her nose was tickling too. Then she sneezed, and a wonderful calm came over her. Her eyes became heavy, and with a sigh she settled back to bed.

Misty woke the next morning feeling surprisingly rested. She smiled to herself as she remembered the cat on her windowsill, and she wondered if he had really spoken to her or if she had imagined it? Since leaving home she frequently had restless nights and when she did sleep her dreams caused her to wake in a pool of sweat. Because of this she often struggled to stay awake in class. Her father had come down on her like a ton of bricks, fed up with the phone calls from Mr Lockwood telling him she had fallen asleep again. However today felt different, but more importantly *she* felt different.

She went to the window and opened the curtains. There was nothing to see apart from the grey tower blocks surrounding the building, but then something caught her eye. There was something on the window ledge outside. She opened the window and picked up a feather the size of her hand, black and glossy with a subtle green-blue sheen. She brought it inside and quickly shut the window as quietly as she could. She held it between her fingers and brushed it against her cheek. It tickled. She sniffed it and it immediately reminded her of home. She could smell apple and cinnamon, maybe some nutmeg too, yes it reminded her of her favourite food, her mum's homemade apple crumble. She sniffed it one more time and shed a tear, then she wiped her eyes and put the feather in her school bag.

While Misty got ready for school, her father was still in bed sleeping off the beer. So, she made herself some breakfast: stale cornflakes and milk, ironed her skirt, combed her hair, and brushed her teeth with just water as they had run out of toothpaste. Then she got herself dressed and decided she would guess the time again. *Eight thirty-three,* she thought and checked the clock on her way out. She smiled to herself; she was definitely on a roll.

CHAPTER 2

 Misty didn't like school. She found it a struggle and she often got told off for daydreaming. Although a naturally bright child, since moving to Willowbrook High School she had struggled to concentrate. Her grades were poor and according to Mr Lockwood the Head Teacher, she wasn't expected to amount to much.

The journey to school was also a struggle. Firstly, there was a fifteen-minute walk to the bus stop, then a ten-minute bus ride which took her close to the school gates. Misty would pass other children laughing and shoving each other, mainly in play, although some of the meaner children would tease the smaller ones, the smarter ones, or the ones that looked, well, different. She would dread this journey and tried to leave home early to avoid the bullies, keeping her head down and her guard up, and hoping she would make it without any trouble.

Since moving to the estate nearly a year ago, she had not found it easy to make friends instead finding herself a target for the bullies, mainly girls but some of the boys too. Although she was tall for her age, she wasn't the tidiest girl. Her clothes were second hand, her hair was a tangled array of unruly ginger curls, which despite her attempts at styling it had a mind of its own, and her teeth needed braces, but her father had not got around to taking her to the dentist. Neither did he encourage her to maintain her appearance, he was too distracted with money, or the lack of it, to bother with such things.

There had been a few scuffles with a particular group of girls who were cruel about her appearance, calling her *ugly* or *weird*, and on more than a few occasions she had been pushed to the point of losing her temper and had struck out. The group of bullies had run off laughing and she had gone home with cuts and bruises, ripped clothes and snotty tear-stained cheeks. With nobody at home to guide or comfort her it was becoming harder to cope with, which made her miss her mum and brother even more.

However, today she found herself skipping along and humming a tune to herself, a tune she had never heard before and yet she had woken up with it in her head, and it was an ear worm she couldn't get rid of. She got off the bus distracted, humming the tune and didn't notice the small group of boys casually walking together in front of her until she bumped into one of them, almost knocking him over.

Oops, sorry," she said as she moved quickly out of the way, bracing herself for an altercation, until she realised it was Charlie.

Charlie was her neighbour and he had been really friendly to her since she moved in, she almost considered him a friend.

"You seem happy today!" he said, his toothy grin gleaming. "What's happened? Won the lottery or something?" They always liked to talk about what they would do if they won loads of money, getting away from the estate was first on their list.

"Ha! I wish!" She said with a smile, then she realised she was already at the school gates although she couldn't remember getting there. "I just have a good feeling about today, wanna race?" She said, nudging his arm. They both bolted to the main door, the other kids moving sideways to let them pass, Misty got there first and stood there panting and smiling until Charlie caught up.

"Cheat," he said with a smile.

"Bad loser," she said back, both giggling and trying to catch their breath.

"OI! cut it out you two, no running in the yard!" They heard the headteacher Mr Lockwood shout sternly.

"Catch you at break, Mystery." Charlie said as he winked at her and quickly headed to class. Mystery was his nickname for her, which seemed to suit her as he claimed she didn't give much away.

It was true that she didn't talk about herself, she'd rather not, but that didn't seem to matter as they had a few things in common. They both lived in the same neighbourhood and shared a similar twisted sense of humour, and they liked to race.

First lesson was biology. Misty wasn't a fan but did enjoy some of it. She showed a natural affinity with animals, apart from rats. Misty hated rats, they made her skin crawl and the thought of their snaky tails, eugh! They were nasty.

"Today children, we will be learning about evolution, including natural and artificial selection" announced Miss Grim, biology's dullest teacher, ever. *Grim by name, Grim by nature* she thought, a term she had picked up from Charlie, he was so funny, she chuckled to herself.

As Miss Grim proceeded to inform the class about the "marvellous Mister Darwin," she found herself thinking about the mysterious experience of last night. The cat sat on her windowsill, black as night, with those sparkly green eyes. *What was his name? That's right, Shadow,* she smiled to herself, *yes, he talked, actually talked! He said he had something for me.* Then she remembered the feather. As she sat there daydreaming, she wondered if she might be going a bit crazy. She hadn't been sleeping that well lately and maybe it was making her see things. She'd heard the doctors who took her mum away say she was mentally ill. What if she was too? *No, it definitely happened, I'm not mad,* she thought.

Waiting for Miss Grim to turn her back she rummaged in her bag, there it was! She rubbed it between her fingers and sniffed,

"Apple crumble! Yes, Shadow left me a pudding smelling feather." She muttered quietly, then as she did something caught the corner of her eye.

She turned toward the window nearest to her, then a gust of wind rattled the glass and an old woman, clear as crystal, in a costume so bizarre that she couldn't quite take it in, flew past on a broomstick. The old woman looked directly into Misty's eyes and winked, a big beaming smile across her face and a big black cat, with sparkly green eyes, sat on her lap. She blinked and they were gone. She was so shocked that she shrieked, her chair toppled over, and she landed on the floor in a heap.

"Misty Morgan! Get up from there. Disrupting the class again. Well, I won't tolerate it, get to Mr Lockwood's office right now!" Shouted Miss Grim.

She got up and made for the door as fast as her feet would carry her.

"Sorry Miss Grim," she said half-heartedly, and was straight down the corridor and outside Mr Lockwood's office in record time.

She sat outside his office wondering if anyone else had seen that strange sight. She remembered that it was nearly Halloween, but surely it was too early for witch costumes. Her heart was still fluttering when he called her in, but she wasn't that worried about seeing him as she'd been there twenty times already this term. As usual she was greeted by Mr Lockwood who was sat behind a larger than average antique desk.

"Greetings Misty Morgan, sit down and tell me what's happened this time. No don't tell me, let me guess. Disrupting class again?" He said. "This is becoming a regular thing now, tell me, are things alright at home?" He sounded concerned rather than angry, which surprised her.

She wasn't sure what to say, so she stumbled over her words in a way that almost sounded convincing. "Mmm, yes, no, I mean, everything is fine, sorry Sir ... I mean ..." Then a gust of wind rattled Mr Lockwood's window, more fiercely than before and caused the curtain to flutter. She looked and saw the same old woman again, sat on a broomstick with the black cat on her lap, and this time she was playing a flute. She could hear the same tune she had been humming earlier that day, then they disappeared.

Mr Lockwood also looked through the window, at the same time as Misty, as it seemed that he too had heard the wind and seen the curtain flutter. But all he saw was a crow flying past, black, like the feather she had found on her windowsill.

"Right, where were we? Ah yes, Miss Grim rang to tell me you've been disrupting class again, causing a ruckus by falling off your chair ... mmm yes, are you alright dear? Do you need to see Nurse Allgood?" He seemed distracted and hardly noticed Misty's wide eyes, open mouth and jaw practically on the floor.

"No, I'm fine Sir, nothing hurting anyway," she replied without thinking.

"Right, what shall we do with you? I know, those rat cages in the biology class need cleaning, just the job, don't you agree?" He said with a perplexed look on his face.

"Yes Sir, I totally agree," she replied, not yet realising what she was agreeing to.

"Right, after school, see Miss Grim and she can show you the ropes, now off you go," said Mr Lockwood in a tone that seemed, well, disinterested. On leaving the room she glanced back and saw he was looking at something out of the window. *He saw her too,* she was sure he had, *I can't be mad.*

She left Mr Lockwood's office as quickly as she arrived, feeling slightly unnerved by the whole thing, now that the punishment had sunk in. She'd been expecting detention but not that!

"Rats!" She muttered, "I hate rats." She headed back to class still thinking about the old woman and feeling quite lightheaded.

CHAPTER 3

Detention after school was a harsh punishment for the kids who had nice homes to go to. Some, however, didn't have much to look forward to when the end of school bell rang, Misty included. But things hadn't always been that way. Before her mum's illness they had a comfortable and happy life in the country. Mum would read them stories, make beautiful puddings, and her father would play games with them. He rarely shouted back then, and her favourite memory was when he made them a tree house in the garden. More importantly she couldn't ever remember feeling frightened.

Today had started out so well but had gradually got weirder and weirder. She would have preferred to run ten laps around the playing field than clean out the rat cages. It would not be a pleasant task, even for those who didn't mind the furry, bitey creatures with snakes for tails. She had met Charlie at break time and told him about her punishment, but she held back on telling him the full story. She didn't want him to think she was mad, even though she was starting to think so.

The school bell rang, and all the children left for home, apart from Misty who made her way to the biology classroom. Miss Grim was waiting for her, miserable as usual, and without a word between them she took her through to a room beyond the classroom; a place which was usually out of bounds. She had already seen inside that dreaded room, well, at least a glimpse. A few months ago, she snuck a peak when Miss Grim was otherwise engaged with a fainting pupil, which happened during the dissection of a toad. Fiona was the pupil, and she never lived that down. From then on, she was "Fragile Fiona" and had to put up with jibes about toads. Toby McLeod even brought in a live one he had caught from his garden and put it in her bag. Poor Fragile Fiona spent the rest of the day in Nurse Allgood's office. Anyway, whist Fragile Fiona was stretched out on the classroom floor she had taken the opportunity to quench her desire for what lay beyond, and it scared the life out of her. Smelly cages with locusts, test tubes, bottles with strange, coloured liquids, containers with unknown dead stuff inside, fridges full of dead animals and the rats. Stinky, scratchy rats. Now she was back, and this time it wasn't down to her curiosity.

"You don't need to get the rats out Misty, just change the bedding, and water ... and give them food," said Miss Grim, "... and don't get up to any mischief," she added on her way out.

The door slammed shut and she was alone in the room of terror, at least she thought she was alone. She looked around and shuddered. The room was quite dark, and she could hear flicking noises coming from the locust tanks. The rat cages were in front of her, there were five or six, or maybe a hundred rats in there, she didn't care.

Misty stood there staring into space for a minute or two, trying to muster up the courage to approach them when she heard a gust of wind blowing one of the windows. It rattled and the wind seemed to blow right through her, and her wispy red hair tickled her forehead. Then something moved in the shadows, and she saw a dark figure in the corner of her eye. Misty turned to see, but there was nothing there. She turned back to the rat cages and her heart stopped. She froze, and her neck prickled as she saw the shadows move again.

"Hello Misty," said the figure emerging from behind the cages. There before her was the old woman she had seen flying past the windows earlier that day. She closed her eyes for a moment, hoping she was a figment of her imagination. She opened her eyes, and the woman was still there, smiling at her.

The old woman had a kindly face, white hair tidied into two long braids, a purple pointed hat and matching cloak. Misty looked her up and down, trying to make sense of who stood before her. She could smell that distinctive smell of apple crumble and noticed she was wearing green stripey tights, big black boots and was holding a broomstick that was taller than she was. Black feathers were stuck loosely to her cloak, some had already fallen around her feet and on her boots. The woman shook each foot in turn and the feathers scattered across the floor. Misty could just about make out a flute, poking out of a tatty old bag, and hanging sloppily off her shoulder.

"Er, hello?" Misty said, trying desperately to stand her ground, and not to turn and run straight out of there. But her legs were feeling quite wobbly and the prickles on her neck were still there. "W … w … who are y … you?" She stammered.

The woman looked at her and Misty had a feeling they had met before.

"Don't you remember?" Said the woman and she took out her flute and played. It sounded like wind whistling down a chimney, or through a badly fitted window.

"Is it Windy?" Misty asked. It was the first word that popped into her head.

"No, but close," said the woman, "It's Wendy," and she laughed. She laughed in a way that was so appealing and warm that Misty immediately felt calm. She joined in and they laughed together for what seemed like ages.

"You've already met Shadow," said Wendy and coughed, as if to prompt him. Then, from behind the curtain the black fluffy cat with sparkling green eyes emerged. He nodded his head as if to say hello and then jumped up onto the locust tank, making himself comfortable next to the heat lamp, closed his eyes, yawned, and went to sleep.

Judging by her arrival on a broomstick Misty guessed that Wendy was a witch. She wondered what she wanted with her and why this was happening, but she didn't care to ask. She felt excited and for some reason she trusted this peculiar woman who seemed so familiar to her and eagerly took instructions from her on what to do.

As Misty opened the first cage Wendy started playing her flute and she recognised it immediately as the same tune she'd been humming on her way to school. The rats came out of their cage, mesmerised by the sound of the flute, and one by one sat happily on her wide brimmed hat whilst Misty proceeded to clean out the cages. There were three cages in total, and she counted thirteen rats.

"I don't want to lose any of you," she said gently to them, and they twitched their noses and squeaked.

Before long the cages were clean, water bottles filled, and food bowls restocked with unappetising looking rodent pellets. Wendy stopped playing and each rat, one by one, obediently went back into their home. Misty clipped the cages shut and looked up at Wendy, who was putting her flute back in her bag.

"Well done, Misty, well done," she said enthusiastically and patted her on the shoulder. "I have to go now, come Shadow," and with that a big gust of wind rattled the window and they were gone.

"But ..." Misty called, "will I see you again?" she heard no reply but the distant sound of whistling wind.

Feeling exhilarated she returned to the classroom where Miss Grim was sat at her desk, she looked up and eyed her with suspicion.

"What do you want child?" She looked at the clock on the wall facing her. "You can't be finished it's only ..." Misty looked at the clock. She'd only been five minutes, but it seemed like an hour had passed.

"Yes, Miss Grim, all done," she said, looking quite pleased with herself.

Miss Grim scowled and muttered "Impossible!" under her breath. She scraped her chair back from her desk and marched through to the back room. Misty waited, smiling to herself. Miss Grim returned with a crooked smile on her stern face.

"Well Misty, I must say I'm very impressed. Job well done; I've never seen such clean cages." Miss Grim didn't often give complements and Misty felt really pleased with herself.

She left school feeling unusually happy. The past twenty-four hours had been strange, but unbelievably wonderful and she felt like she was walking on air. She wasn't that late leaving either so was able to catch her usual bus. The driver grinned at her as she got on.

"Welcome aboard," he said and winked.

"Er thanks," she said in reply and sat in her usual seat. She could see him staring at her in the mirror and poked her tongue out at him. *What's he looking at?* She thought and stared out of the window.

"See you soon Misty," he said as she got off. *How does he know my name?* She thought.

"Yes, see you soon Rudy," she replied without thinking. *How do I know his name? Today is really strange,* she thought as she made her way back home.

Her father was in his bedroom when she arrived. The walls were thin and although his door was closed, she could hear him talking on the phone and every now and then he would curse loudly. She tried to be as quiet as possible and tiptoed to the kitchen, made herself some buttered toast, and poured herself a glass of milk. She flopped wearily on the sofa and smiled to herself. The television was on the blink, so she got out her notebook. *Hmm, I think I'll start a diary,* and proceeded to write down the events of the day, so she wouldn't forget.

"Misty!" She heard her father call her from his room, her heart sank. "What's for supper?" He asked. He was not a great cook, and since the upheaval of moving out of the family home he had relied on her for many things, including feeding him. Misty wandered into the kitchen and opened the fridge. There wasn't much in there, just a few eggs, and a stale piece of cheese, she had used up all the milk but then remembered there were a few slices of bread left in the bread bin. She made them both a cheese sandwich, then wrapped up some scraps and put them in her school blazer pocket. *For the rats.*

CHAPTER 4

Keeping a diary wasn't popular amongst her peers. The only person she knew that had kept one was her mum and she had often seen her writing in it. She had kept it hidden and Misty had longed to see what was in it. She would wonder if her mother was writing about her, maybe she wrote that she was upset with her when she'd been naughty, maybe she wrote that she loved Michael more than her, or that she was really adopted; the list in her head went on, feeding on her insecurities.

Just before Mum was taken away, she had been so upset and angry by the goings on that she decided to soothe herself with mischief. Having a curious nature, she took it upon herself to sneak into her parents' bedroom and snoop around. It was then that she came upon the diary, in the drawer of Mum's bedside table. It was a brown leather-bound book, with strange symbols on the cover, and it smelled like her best buckled boots. The temptation to look inside was too much for Misty and without any hesitation she picked it up and let the pages fall open on their own, using fate as an indicator of what she would discover. She regretted it almost immediately, she had only read a few pages when her brother

Michael crept up behind her and whispered creepily in her ear.

"Caught you!"

She dropped the diary and pushed him away.

"You beast," she yelled at him, and the diary fell.

Pages came loose and it was ruined by the pair of them wrestling with each other on the floor, accidentally kicking it around as their feet collided with each other. Their father, alerted by the ruckus, came, and separated them. The memory of their mum stood by the door with tears rolling down her cheeks made her sad, even now. It was the first time Misty had learnt that some things should be kept private.

It was Misty who was punished for that one. No television for two weeks, although she did admit it was kind of deserved. She promised never to snoop anywhere again, a promise she knew she could never keep, and she had her fingers crossed when she said it. Although, those few pages that she had read meant nothing to her at the time, it was like garbled nonsense. She felt disappointed, but really, she was too young to understand what those secrets were about.

Since her separation from her mother and brother, Misty had tried to remember the good times. But it was getting harder and more recently she had become more preoccupied with negative thoughts. She wondered if Mum's illness was her fault. She wondered if she'd been too much of a nuisance. She wondered that if she had been good, then maybe Mum might not have been taken away. Michael might not have gone to live with Aunt Bella, and she wouldn't be stuck in this horrible dreary flat with her drunken father, and no room to call her own.

Today felt different. She felt energetic and excited and didn't want to think about anything that would bring her down. She remembered telling herself that one day she would have her own diary, and write down her own secrets, and today was the day. She grinned, grabbed the keys from Dad's secret tin and headed down to the lock-up in the basement of the building. She ran down the twenty flights of stairs as the lift took far too long and stunk of pee. She pushed through the gate and skittered around the back of the building and down the final two flights of stairs. At last, the special room which kept her precious things. Well, really it contained all their things, as there wasn't much room in the flat for anything more than essentials.

She turned the key and the door sprung open; her eyes met with boxes piled high. Most were labelled with *Mr Robert Morgan* but some of them had her name scribbled on the side with black marker. She tried not to feel overwhelmed by the boxes, a year had passed since she'd seen them, and she wracked her brain to remember which box she needed without having to open each one. She had to find that special book, the one given to her one Christmas by Aunt Bella; an extremely heavy leather-bound book that wasn't dissimilar to her mum's diary.

The diary hunt turned out to be quite interesting. Not only did she find the diary, but also a selection of items that she had totally forgotten about, like her battered old karaoke machine, a pack of antique playing cards, and a chemistry set, all of which also happened to be presents from Aunt Bella. She decided to lug them all back up to the flat, hiding them under the sofa in case her father objected.

Later that evening, feeling tired but still enthusiastic, she waited for her father to go to bed before she brought out the leather-bound book. She sniffed it; the smell reminded her of home. *I wonder what happened to my best buckled boots?* She thought wistfully. She opened the book, turned to the first page, and started to write, firstly putting the date at the top, and then she began with *'The day I met Wendy ...'*

She wrote down all the details she could remember. She never wanted to forget, as it felt like something important was happening for her at last. She closed the book and settled herself down to sleep, placing it under her pillow. Misty could hear the clock ticking in the hallway.

"I guess, hmm, eleven fifty-five," she said quietly. She had just enough energy to creep out of bed and check, and the two arrows were on the eleven. She was dead on, third time in a row.

Misty snuggled up in bed still smiling and drifted into a peaceful slumber. That night her dreams were vivid, if a little jumbled up. The following morning, she tried to make some sense of them but as the morning went by the more the dreams evaporated, like dreams do. She could remember being on the top of a high mountain, looking around and seeing nothing but the tops of trees. There were birds, black like the feather she kept in her school bag, and she could hear them cawing, seemingly, wanting her to follow them. She thought she might have heard one speak, but she couldn't quite recall. Maybe she did follow them?

"I flew with them, yes I jumped on the back of a bird and flew!" She said out loud. Feeling so satisfied that she didn't even notice that her father was speaking to her.

"Misty, MISTY!" His voice jarred her current serenity.

"Oh, sorry Dad," she said apologetically.

"Time to go to school. Don't forget I won't be here when you get home, I'll be at The King Arthur," he said. She wasn't bothered about being alone, she could please herself and didn't have to prepare his supper. As long as she was asleep by the time he got home everything would be fine.

"No problem," she answered, and grabbing her coat and bag, she left the flat earlier than usual, hoping she would bump into Charlie.

CHAPTER 5

It was a crisp autumn morning. The sun shone golden hues, and orange and red leaves fluttered to the ground, blown by the soft breeze. Misty playfully kicked the piles of leaves which had been carefully swept to the sides of the path by the school caretaker, whilst noticing that smell in the air. It reminded her of her favourite time of year, Halloween. She had loved dressing up in ghoulish costumes and going door to door with Mum and Michael, collecting sweets from the neighbours. She longed for her old life and missed her mum and brother more than ever.

"Mystery!" She heard Charlie call her from across the yard. He came running over panting.

"I've got some news," he said trying to catch his breath. "I'm having a Halloween party this weekend, fancy coming?" He looked at her, eyes wide in anticipation.

"Sure," she said, "I'll ask my dad. He'll probably say no, but I'll come anyway," she said with a shrug, secretly over the moon but trying not to show it.

Charlie grinned his big toothy smile.

"Don't forget its fancy dress!" He shouted back at her as he ran off to his maths lesson.

Weird, I was just thinking about Halloween, she thought as she wandered over to join the line for Biology.

There was a group of popular girls huddled together sniggering, they had obviously overheard and started to make fun.

"You won't have to wear fancy dress, you could go as you are, freak!" Said Emily, a popular girl who was pretty, but not particularly nice and had picked on Misty since her first day at the school. The other girls laughed and pointed at her. Misty felt something go off inside her, like a bomb. Her heart pounded and she started to shake. Emily continued.

"Hahaha, with clothes like those you could go as a ..." but before she could finish her sentence Misty felt a rage inside her that she couldn't control and without warning she struck Emily, who fell backwards into the other girls, who in turn caught her, and pushed her back up. Misty stood there staring Emily in the face, fist ready and waiting for her to come at her. She could hear people shouting and screaming but it was too late to back off now, she had to finish it.

Misty couldn't recall what happened next, everything went black, then she heard a voice whisper in her ear.

"Misty, open your eyes." She did. She thought she must be dead as all she could see was swirling yellow and white light surrounding a beautiful face, which she thought must belong to an angel. She tried to focus but the light just got brighter, and she felt a warm fluttering sensation in her stomach.

"Where am I? Am I in heaven?" She asked the angel.

"It's ok, you're safe now," was the reply. She felt arms around her that helped her to her feet, the arms felt strong, and they raised her up with ease. She blinked her eyes, the light started to dim, and her eyes became focused. There, standing in front of her was Fragile Fiona.

"Fiona? Is that you?" She asked.

Misty felt confused, she was stood in the line with the other children who were now staring at her with a mixture of suspicion and awe. Emily was brushing herself down with the other girls fussing over her and nobody was saying a word.

"What just happened?" Misty whispered to Fiona, "did I hit her?"

Fiona placed an arm gently around her shoulder and whispered back.

"Sort of, but you didn't actually touch her, she just fell back, that's all. Don't worry, she won't be picking on you again, I'm sure of that."

Nobody said a word for the whole lesson, the children were perfectly quiet and well behaved, which made a change. However, it didn't seem that they were listening to anything that Miss Grim was teaching them as they were just trying to get their heads around what had just happened. The class had witnessed something quite extraordinary, having seen Misty Morgan knock Emily off her feet without even touching her; it was, well, unbelievable. Misty was also struggling to understand what had happened as it seemed too bizarre for her to comprehend. She wondered if Wendy would be able to shed some light on the situation. If only she could bring Wendy back again, she could ask her. She needed a plan, and by the end of the lesson she had one.

After class Misty approached Miss Grim, who was busying herself shuffling papers on her desk.

"I was wondering Miss if I could look after the rats again? Or help in any other way, maybe the locusts need feeding?" She asked, trying to sound sincere.

Miss Grim looked up, her eyes sparkled, and her lips contorted to what resembled a smile. She had never seen Miss Grim smile, she only seemed to have one face, and that was stern.

"Well, well, Misty Morgan." She said looking her up and down. "I wouldn't have put you down as the helpful type." She took a deep breath.

"Yes, I suppose you could help me look after things back there, there's lots to do mind you, I hope you're up for a challenge?" She released her breath, looked down at the desk and carried on shuffling papers.

"Meet me here at the end of the day and I'll show you what to do," she said without looking up.

Word spread like wildfire around the school. By lunchtime everyone was talking about Misty Morgan flooring Emily with just her mind, and she was fast becoming everyone's topic of gossip. Misty wasn't sure how to deal with all the whispering and stares, so she went in search of Charlie, but despite her searching he was nowhere to be found.

Feeling lonely and vulnerable she found herself distracted by thoughts of Wendy and was determined to see her again, so she really needed her plan to work.

Miss Grim was surprised to see Misty walk through the door at the end of school and seemed genuinely pleased. Firstly, she congratulated her on showing an interest and then insisted on talking her through the procedure again. Misty didn't think it was necessary but went along with it, mainly to humour her, but also not to disappoint her; Miss Grim seemed to take great pleasure in showing her the ins and the outs of the biology storeroom. Eventually the door closed, and Misty was alone. Feeling a little bit queasy with excitement, she decided to get straight to work as 'time was of the essence,' another expression she had picked up from Charlie.

He was so smart.

Misty made her way to the rat cages. She could hear them scratching and squeaking but this time she wasn't bothered. She closed her eyes and concentrating on seeing Wendy's face in her mind's eye, she whispered her name.

"Wendy?" She opened her eyes hoping she would be stood in front of her, but there were just a few rats poking their long twitchy noses through the bars and nothing else. She closed her eyes and said it again.

"Wendy!" She opened one eye this time, but nothing. *This is stupid,* she thought, but decided to try one last time.

"Third time lucky," she said to the rats, then loudly and firmly she said

"WENDY!"

She felt a surge of energy rising from her feet and out through her fingers. She kept her eyes firmly shut and could hear a rattling noise coming from the window, then a rustling. Her stomach churned and she felt a tingling sensation throughout her body. The rustling noise got louder and then she felt a breeze which turned to wind, then a warm gust blew the hair from off her face. Frozen to the spot she stood with her arms by her sides and her fingers outstretched. Then the wind and the rattling stopped. She heard music, she recognised the tune, her heart was beating fast, and the tingling sensation intensified. She knew she was there but was too scared to open

34

her eyes, in case - just in case - she had imagined it all.

"You can open your eyes now Misty." She recognised the soft sing song tone of Wendy's voice. "I've been waiting," she said.

Misty opened one eye, then the other and right before her stood Wendy, who was shaking off the black feathers that were clinging to her. She stood boldly holding her broomstick in one hand and the other stretched out toward her. Misty wasn't sure what to do, whether to shake her hand, run for the door or faint on the spot. Instead, she threw her arms around Wendy's broad shoulders and held her close to her, just for a moment, as if she needed confirmation, that she was real and not an apparition.

Wendy felt warm and her clothes smelt of apple crumble. Her platted hair tickled Misty's neck and she could feel her chest heaving, like she was struggling to breathe. Misty let go and Wendy gasped and then chuckled.

"Summerland's above! You've got a mighty big grip," she said.

"I called to you, and you came!" Misty shrieked, shaking like a leaf.

"Of course, you did," said Wendy softly. "You knew that if you needed me enough you could bring me here. Now, what do you need me for?" She looked her straight in the eyes, "Well?"

Misty had no idea how to respond, she hadn't thought this bit through at all, she had just wanted to know if she was real and now, she felt confused, and a little silly.

"Who are you? Are you my fairy godmother or something?" She said feeling even sillier. Wendy took her by the hand and chuckled.

"I suppose I should introduce myself properly. My name is Wendy, and I am a witch." She let go of Misty's hand, curtsied, and bowed her head, "I am very old, older than you can imagine, and I've been watching over you since you were born, waiting for you to be ready."

Then she clicked her fingers and Shadow emerged from behind the curtain. He trotted confidently toward Misty and sat down, staring at her with his green sparkly eyes.

"Ready for what?" asked Misty.

"For your destiny," said Wendy. "There is much to learn, much to see and do, and I will guide you, if you will let me," she added. Misty nodded.

"When do we start?" She asked.

"We start now," said Wendy with a smile.

CHAPTER 6

From as far back as she could remember Misty loved reading fairy tales, but unlike other girls of her age she would sometimes feel sorry for the witch. That didn't mean that she was wicked like the witches were often portrayed in the stories. She was in fact, a very kind girl and always tried to see the best in everyone, even the villains. It was her father who had instilled this value, telling her that sometimes people were portrayed as bad because they were misunderstood, or feared because they were different. Now she was in the presence of a witch, a real live witch, and so far, she had no reason to believe she was bad. So, until proven otherwise she would continue to believe her good.

Misty had many questions for Wendy. she wanted to know where she came from, how she could fly, why she had chosen her, but mostly she wanted to know what she meant by her *destiny*. Those questions, however, could wait for now.

They worked quickly, cleaning and feeding the rats and locusts whilst Shadow found a warm spot to sleep. Misty had found the little scraps of bread and cheese in her pocket and gave them to the rats who ate them with delight. She heard them talking with their squeaky little voices *thank you, thank you, thank you*. She watched exactly what Wendy was doing and thought it looked so effortless with her long spindly fingers, light and delicate as though she was playing a piano. She copied her the best she could, and it wasn't long before their work was done, and everything was clean and put away correctly.

She wasn't sure how much time had passed when she heard the door creak open, and Wendy and Shadow quickly hid behind the curtains. Miss Grim strutted toward Misty with her hands on her hips and her nose sniffing the air. She checked the rats, the locusts, the tubs of goo, the dead stuff, the brightly coloured jars and finally checked nothing had been stolen. She knew every inch of that storeroom and she couldn't assume Misty was trustworthy.

"What's that smell? Smells like pudding." Miss Grim said with her large nostrils flaring. She looked confused. "Cats! I can smell cats. Have you seen anything resembling a cat in here?" She said, sniffing the air like a dog in a sausage shop.

Misty knew she had to distract Miss Grim away from discovering her new friends. She could see Wendy's boots and a black bushy tail sticking out from under the curtains, and her big broomstick leaning against the wall. The curtains were made of a thick material, but

Misty could see Wendy's distinctive shape bulging out. Then she thought she heard a faint giggling coming from behind the curtain. *What's she playing at?* She thought, feeling a little annoyed. *Does she want to be caught?*

Miss Grim was now sniffing in the direction of the hiding place.

"Cats and crumble," she muttered to herself. "That's it, apple crumble and cats."

Miss Grim kept repeating this to herself, whilst Misty was thinking of how to distract her. She had to act fast.

"Miss Grrr ..." and before she could finish she crumpled like a deflated balloon on the floor.

"Oh, dear god!" Shrieked Miss Grim as she turned to see Misty, collapsed in a heap. She hurried over, checked her pulse then quickly swept her up into her arms and carried her to Nurse Allgood's office.

Misty was aware of everything, but she pretended to be out of it for as long as she could.

"Misty?" She could hear Nurse Allgood's shrill voice in her ear. She jumped and opened her eyes.

"What just happened?" Misty asked innocently.

"She's fine Margaret," Nurse Allgood reassured Miss Grim.

"Thank goodness Mavis," she replied to Nurse Allgood. Misty found it quite peculiar hearing them call each other by their first names.

"Can I go now, Nurse Allgood?" she asked, getting up from the bed, "I need to get my bag, I left it in the classroom."

She really wanted to go and check on Wendy and Shadow. Nurse Allgood agreed but insisted on escorting her back to the biology room herself, just to make sure she was alright. So, Nurse Allgood took her by the hand, and they headed back, with Miss Grim scuttling behind, still sniffing the air with a look of bewilderment on her face.

When they arrived, the room was quiet and there was no sign of Wendy or Shadow. Everything was in order, and Miss Grim made a point of saying that the funny smell had gone. Nurse Allgood wanted to check Misty over one last time, just to be sure, so she asked her to sit down, while she checked her pupils, pulse, and her temperature.

"All good," she said with a smile and squeezed her hand.

Misty felt a warm tingle rise up from her hand. As she looked at Nurse Allgood, she had a feeling that the nurse knew what was going on. She couldn't put her finger on it, but she knew that she knew. Nurse Allgood gave her a knowing wink, as she left the room. Misty could have sworn she heard her humming the same tune that Wendy had played on her flute. She shook her head and told herself not to be so silly, *that would be too weird.*

When she arrived home, she remembered that her father would be home late. That meant, she didn't have to prepare his supper or run his bath, and she didn't have to stay as quiet as a mouse. She didn't have to *behave;* she could just *be.* She made herself a fish finger sandwich, pulled out her bed, and snuggled up under the duvet to keep warm and think about her day.

The flat was so quiet, all she could hear was the ticking of the grandfather clock in the hall. The sound was mesmerising. She wondered about guessing the time again, could she do it four times in a row? *I guess six thirty-three,* she thought, but rather than get up from her bed she checked her phone which was in her pocket. The time was just changing to six thirty-three. Satisfied, she closed her eyes and snuggled into her pillow. At least she thought it was her pillow, but it was furry, warm, and purring.

"What on ...!" She shrieked, opened her eyes, and looked straight into the sparkly green eyes of Shadow. He was curled up as if he'd been sleeping there a while. He yawned, stretched his legs, and got up, arching his back, the way cats do.

"Where did YOU come from? How did you get in?" She cried.

"You let me in," she heard him say, with his deep silky soft voice, clear as day.

She had no recollection of opening the door or the window, but she wasn't going to worry about that.

"Where's your diary?" She heard him say.

"It's here," she replied, getting it from under the mattress, showing it to him. He rubbed the side of his mouth on the edge of the leather-bound book several times, and it quivered as though it was alive; the pages flicking open and shut. The cover pulsated and strange symbols appeared, shimmering with bright yellow light. Then it stopped. The strange symbols remained on the front cover, as if burned into it, but Misty had no idea what they meant.

She stared at her diary with disbelief. Shadow nudged her with his head and snuggled into her.

"What just happened?" She asked him.

He seemed to ignore her and made himself comfortable again on her pillow. Then he looked at her.

"All that is secret will be discovered." He said.

Misty looked at the book again.

"This is my Book of Shadows," she said firmly to herself, with a sense of knowing without knowing. She had the most peculiar feeling that Shadow had told her this before, but a long time ago.

Misty fell asleep holding her book close to her chest and woke in the morning still clutching it. She looked around. Shadow was nowhere to be seen. Her father was in the kitchen making breakfast. Misty asked herself if it was all a dream and looked at her diary. The symbols were still firmly imprinted on the cover.

"My book of shadows." She whispered under her breath.

CHAPTER 7

All that is secret will be discovered.
The words repeated in Misty's head, which she found strangely comforting. She had no idea what this meant but the possibilities excited her.

She had a spring in her step today, despite the cold rain. With wet leaves beneath her feet she slipped, skidded, and glided over puddles to school. She was almost at the school gate when she remembered a dream she had during the night. It came to her in a flash and then disappeared just as quickly. She tried desperately to remember it, but the images had already evaporated. All that remained was a floating sensation that made her want to soar into the sky and be blown by the wind high up into the clouds. She felt as light as a feather, and before she knew it, she had taken one step, then another and then ran as fast as she could before launching herself upwards. She didn't get far; in fact, she didn't even make it over a puddle before she was soaked from her feet up to her knees.

"Blow it!" She muttered to herself.

She could hear laughing so looked around to see where it was coming from. She saw a large group of children pointing and sniggering. She noticed Charlie was with them and her heart sank. She felt embarrassed that he'd seen her acting foolishly and walked on quickly, but she heard footsteps coming from behind, followed by his familiar chuckle.

"Oi Mystery, wait up," she heard him call, so she slowed down and waited for him.

"You crack me up," he said still chuckling. "Think you're a bird or something? Flapping your arms like you have wings, nutter," he said playfully.

She hadn't even realised she'd done that. She felt heat rise to her cheeks, so she changed the subject.

"So, am I still invited to your party tomorrow?" She asked.

"Wouldn't be a party without you." Charlie said smiling, then he gently nudged her arm and ran back to his friends.

The dream bothered Misty all morning. She had to remember. It was like an itch she had to scratch. Despite this, she still managed to concentrate in class and tried her best to appear interested, even in her worst subject - maths. After lunch was her favourite subject, history. Mr Woolley was her history teacher. He was very ordinary looking, with his grey suit, grey tie, grey beard, and even greyish skin - everything about him was grey, but he had the ability to tell a story so compelling that the lesson was never boring. She liked him very much.

"Today class we are going to learn about the Vikings," said Mr Woolley.

Some of the children in the class cheered as they were attracted to the Vikings fierce reputation, Misty included. They were each given a book that contained pictures and text and instructed to read the first chapter. To her amazement she saw that some of the pictures featured symbols exactly like the ones that appeared on her diary the night before. She read that the symbols were an ancient alphabet called Runes. *What a coincidence* she thought. Then her thoughts were interrupted by Mr Woolley's voice.

"Listen up kids," he said, "I'm going to tell you about an ancient written alphabet used by European's, including the Vikings, called Runes."

Startled, Misty looked up from her book to see him looking at her, his piercing blue eyes gleaming, and he gave her a knowing wink. *No way,* she thought, *this is too incredible.* He went on to teach them the history of the Runes, but what really caught her attention was that they were, and still are considered magical. The name Rune itself translated as 'secret or mystery.' She left school that day with her head spinning and wondering what could possibly happen next.

Misty had the flat to herself again when she got home, so with her father safely out of the way she took out her Book of Shadows. She carefully held it in her hands and felt the Runes beneath her fingers. They felt warm and made her fingertips tingle. Then she had a flash of a memory - it was her mum's diary. It had Runes on it too, Misty was sure of it. She opened her Book of Shadows and started to write.

Misty had just written the date at the top of the page when she was interrupted by a commotion coming from the hallway. The grandfather clock started chiming, and the ticking got louder and louder. Then she heard an almighty crash, followed by, a tumbling sound and then a giggle. She recognised that giggle.

The living room door blew open with an almighty blast of sweet-smelling air, and like a whirlwind Wendy spun across the room before landing on the floor next to her bed. She brushed herself down with her hands and black feathers fell around her feet. Then Misty heard little kitty footsteps padding down the hall and in strutted Shadow. He sat down and yawned showing his sharp white teeth.

"Hello Misty." Wendy and Shadow said in unison.

Although surprised, Misty wasn't frightened. In fact, she was really excited to see them again, and in her home too.

"Can I get you a drink, tea, cola, erm, beer?" She asked, wanting to show she had good manners.

"Thank you my dear, I'll make the tea," answered Wendy, already filling the kettle with water. Wendy opened her tatty old bag and took out what looked like a packet of dried leaves.

"It's tea," she said and tipped them into the teapot.

Whilst waiting for the kettle to boil Wendy wandered around the flat, nosing in each room, sniffing rudely, and picking things up and examining them before putting them back. Misty watched with a puzzled expression.

"Not much to see here," Wendy said obviously unimpressed with the living arrangements. "I can see that life hasn't been easy for you and Robert," she added.

"No, it's horrible here. My father is so sad, and we miss Mum and Michael, and our old home," said Misty, wondering how Wendy knew her father's name.

"I hear you've got a Book of Shadows. Have you used it yet?" Wendy asked whilst pouring the boiling water into the teapot.

"Well, I was about to write in it, but then you appeared. I'm not really sure what it's for," said Misty.

"It's your spell book of course, you must write down all of your magic, so you don't forget it. Here, have some tea," and she handed Misty a steaming cup of herbal tea. It smelled just like

Wendy, like apple crumble. She took a sip and it tasted deliciously unusual.

"Why do I need a spell book?" She asked.

Wendy stopped stirring her tea and looked at Misty.

"I'm so sorry my dear I thought you knew. All witches have spell books!" Misty stared at her in disbelief.

"I'm a witch?"

Wendy dropped her spoon on the floor, and it clattered loudly.

"Oh, cinnamon sticks! It appears I have erred." She said looking quite flustered. "There is much more to do than a thought! Tell me what you *do* know."

Misty looked at her and shook her head.

"Nothing much, I don't think. I know *you* are a witch!"

Wendy sighed. "What about your mum? and Bella?" She asked hopefully, but Misty just looked more confused. "It's alright my dear, we don't have time for this right now, we need to prepare Robert's supper. Hmm, he likes sausages, doesn't he?"

Misty nodded, then they heard a key in the door. It was her father, and with that Wendy and Shadow were gone. Misty was left feeling unexpectedly weary, so she lay down on her bed and closed her eyes.

A warm breeze followed their departure, the window rattled, and the clock chimed, and then her father walked into the living room.

"Misty, I'm home, what's for supper?"

Her father sniffed the air and saw there was a sausage casserole laid out for him on the kitchen table. He smiled for the first time in years as it was his favourite meal.

"Thanks Misty," he said, but she didn't hear him.

She was sound asleep.

CHAPTER 8

While her father was tucking into his sausage casserole, Misty had drifted into a deep sleep. She was in a faraway land, drifting over oceans, mountains, and treetops. There were birds surrounding her, black birds, cawing, dipping, and soaring and looking at her knowingly. She was being taken to a land beyond the realm of her reality. That's all she knew.

As she drifted along with the birds she could hear music, the same tune was being played over and over. It was soothing and melodic, like an orchestra of wind instruments. She hummed along and began to let go of any fears she may have had, opening her arms, and soaring like the birds. She felt different and saw that instead of arms she too had wings, black and shimmering, green-blue, feathers stretching out further than where her fingertips would normally be.

She flapped her wings and went higher. She could see the other birds following her as she navigated the sky, soaring up and diving down. Misty heard them chattering about her, the cawing turned into words and, she understood what they were saying. She heard them say her name and it was then she knew for sure that she too was a crow. This realisation changed the course of the dream. She no longer felt like she was dreaming, it felt as real as everything she did when she was awake. A surge of panic coursed through her veins, and she heard a booming noise in her ears, it felt like her heart was beating so fast it would explode. Then someone called her name.

She could see the other crows, she guessed about twelve in total. They were gathering and heading towards a hilltop not too far away from them. She noticed a circle of large stones and the crows appeared to be heading toward them. She followed, slowing down her pace and gently gliding to a stop on the ground. As she landed, she felt her legs again and looked down to see her feet, no longer those of a crow. She wiggled her toes and shook her arms, touched her nose, and ran her fingers through her hair. Yes, she was a girl again. She shook her body and saw black feathers gather by her feet. When she looked up, she saw Wendy, who was looking directly into her eyes and smiling.

"Misty, you have come further than I hoped. This is wonderful. Now let me introduce you to the others," she said.

She looked around and saw eleven black crows hopping toward her. They stopped and she watched as they started to transform into people, similar black feathers falling around their feet as they too shook themselves back to their human forms. She recognised three of them straight away, Mr Woolley and Mavis Allgood! Fiona LeFey, "Fragile Fiona!" She said out loud. Misty couldn't believe it. Fiona smiled at her and gave her a wave. She thought she must still be dreaming so she pinched herself - it hurt. No! She was definitely awake. There were other people in the group she knew, and the others looked familiar, but it was too much to take in. She took a moment to calm herself down and gather her thoughts.

Wendy beckoned Misty to join them. She stood between Fiona and Mavis and joined hands with them to form a circle with Wendy in the middle. She seemed to be in charge and was holding what looked like a wand in her right hand, she used it to point at each person when it was their turn to speak. They were all dressed in similar outfits, cloaks and pointed hats but all in different colours, and each held a broom with different brightly coloured ribbons wrapped around the handles. They introduced themselves and welcomed her to their group.

"Are you *all* witches?" Misty asked. They all smiled and nodded. As well as Fiona, Mavis Allgood and Mr Woolley, whose first name she found out was Albert, there was Mrs Murphy, who owned the sweet shop by the school. Misty bought her favourite rainbow sherbet from her, and she sold the best gob stoppers around. Then there was the bus driver, Rudy. She remembered that he'd said that he'd *"see me soon,"* but she'd never have guessed this! Then there was Sami Singh a young postman who delivered the mail to her address. And lovely Kitty Bloom, she was a dinner lady at the school, a rather plump lady who always gave Misty extra-large portions of pudding. There was Eli, a large, bearded man with tattoos, and when he smiled he showed a missing front tooth and spoke with a lisp. She'd seen him riding his Harley Davidson motorbike many times. Then, there was Myla McDuff, an attractive lady with scarlet lipstick and piercing green eyes, she was a dance teacher at the local theatre school. Also, the school librarian Ariana White, she always looked serious. Misty was a little scared of her after she told her to "shush" a few months back when she was talking rather loudly to Charlie as they flicked through the comics. Lastly there was Jabir the barber, he regularly cut her father's hair, she remembered he would give her a lollipop and tell jokes while she waited for him.

There were twelve of them in the circle, with Wendy in the centre making thirteen. Thirteen witches, male and female, young and old, all stood together within the stone circle on the hill. She couldn't quite believe what was happening, so she pinched herself again, it still hurt so she knew it was still real. She also noticed something else that was different to any other dream, she could smell the sweet smell of apples, it was wafting over the group and seemed to be emanating from Wendy.

The thirteen witches started to walk slowly, clockwise, in a circle, gradually picking up their pace until they spun around so fast that Misty's stomach flipped over. Then, Wendy brought out her flute and played. Misty recognised the tune immediately and started to hum along. The others joined in and soon they were humming and dancing together, arm in arm for what seemed like hours, but could have been only minutes, as Misty no longer had any concept of time.

As they danced, Misty looked around and saw colourful, sparkly lights rising from Wendy's flute as she played. The lights swirled around the witches like a kaleidoscope of snowflakes. Then, Wendy stopped playing and there was a moment of complete silence. Misty felt excited and energised. She didn't want it to end, she had never felt so happy.

However, the end did come. The colourful sparkly lights disappeared into the night sky, and they all dropped their hands. Misty turned to Fiona and smiled. Fiona smiled back and as she did, her whole body shimmered with iridescent pink and orange colours. Misty had so many questions, but Fiona put her finger to her lips before she even had the chance to ask.

"It is time." Wendy said.

"Will I see you all again?" Misty asked hopefully. They all nodded and blew her a kiss.

She watched as they transformed into crows and flew off into the distance.

Only a moment had passed, and Misty was back home in bed. She sat bolt upright and gasped, trying to catch her breath. The only light was coming in the window, from the moon showing itself as it passed between the clouds. It was full and bright with silver shimmers turning everything a blueish hue. Everything was as she had left it and she could hear the clock ticking loudly in the hall.

Misty got up and tiptoed to the bathroom. She could hear her father snoring in the next room and for some reason she felt comforted by that. Although he could be angry and mean, he was still her father, and at that moment she loved him very much, and she knew he loved her too, even if he didn't always show it. She would not think of her mother, she could not bear it right now. So, as usual, she put her memory back in the box she kept inside her mind and closed the lid.

When she got back to bed, Misty took out her Book of Shadows and wrote everything down, all the details of the night. She couldn't forget, she mustn't. Contented, she fell back to sleep, this time a deep, dreamless sleep.

CHAPTER 9

The next day was Saturday and Misty woke early feeling refreshed and excited. She read again the events of last night, that she had written in her Book of Shadows. This made her feel satisfied that she would never forget, plus she had included Wendy's big revelation that she, herself, was a witch! She didn't feel like a witch. She looked in the mirror and didn't think she looked like one either. She thought that Wendy might be mistaken and yet the dream of the witches at the stone circle had felt so real. Misty needed to find out more, but, decided that she wouldn't worry just yet. Besides, it was Halloween, and she had the party to prepare for.

Misty remembered when she was a little girl, her mum had made a big fuss on Halloween. She remembered her bringing the decorations down from the loft and fighting with Michael over who would hang the glow in the dark skeletons from the big oak tree in the garden. She helped her mum dress the windows with ghosts and cobwebs, and they'd carve a pumpkin. She remembered lighting the candle and placing the snaggle toothed orange monster on the doorstep.

She had not celebrated Halloween since she was seven. She knew this for sure because Mum and Michael had gone away by then, and her father didn't want to celebrate it after that. He would turn the lights off and tell her to pretend they weren't at home. Now, looking back it seemed that Halloween was a particularly sad time for her father so she decided that she wouldn't tell him about Charlie's party. She couldn't risk him stopping her from going. Instead, she would wait until he was back from the pub, having had his fill of beer and whiskey, and was passed out on his bed surrounded by fish and chip wrappers. Then, she would sneak out.

It was a crisp autumn day, there were no trees to be seen from the grubby window of the tower block, so she imagined them with beautiful orange and red leaves shimmering in the sunlight. She opened the window and sniffed the air. It smelled of Halloween and the damp, decaying, but sweet smell triggered even more memories. The good days when Dad was happy. When she was back at home with Mum and Michael, playing in their garden full of beautiful ash, apple, and hawthorn trees, and the one huge oak tree that was about five hundred years old—or so Mum said. She had so many happy memories of climbing that old oak. *What was he called?* She tried hard to recall the name she gave him, for the tree was a '*he*;' Mum had also told her that. She could kick herself for thinking of her again—and Michael. She thought she'd closed that box. *What was his name? Arghhh!*

She slammed the window shut in temper, causing the glass to rattle in the frame. Then, she heard her father rouse from his bedroom and her heart sank. The stomping and vibrating of the floorboards indicated he was heading her way, so she braced herself.

"What have I told you about the windows, stay away from them! If I catch you opening them again you'll see the four corners!" He screeched at her.

He stood by the living room door staring at her with his eyes like daggers, blood shot and bleary. His hair was tousled and, his clothes filthy and torn, and the strong smell of stale beer overpowered the already malodorous flat. She watched, frozen in fear as he staggered toward her with his fist in the air. Not knowing what could, or would happen next, she instinctively looked at the footstool in the corner of the room and watched it moving toward him. The next thing she knew, he missed his footing, tripped over the footstool, and caught his toe. Her father cried out in pain and slumped down on the armchair holding his foot in agony, blood dripping from a split toenail.

"How the devil did that get there?" He said wincing.

She had no idea either. She had just watched it move across the floor on its own.

"It's alright Dad, I'll get you a bandage, and a cup of tea," she said helpfully but also feeling unnaturally responsible for the footstool with a mind of its own.

Her father calmed down after several cups of tea and a peanut butter sandwich, and he told her that he was sorry. Misty knew he meant it, well at least for now, but once he'd had a good drink again, well, who knew. She just hoped that he would leave her alone for the rest of the day so she could plan her costume for the party. He went back to bed, and Misty took the opportunity to search around for something to wear. She found some bin liners and scissors, some string and some sticky tape and got to work.

This is useless, she thought, looking at the scraps of black plastic held together with tape and feeling just a little embarrassed by her feeble attempt. Then a lightbulb turned on in her head. She remembered something. She cleared away the mess, found the basement key in her father's 'not so secret' secret tin, and headed down to the lock-up.

The boxes in the lock-up were piled high and she spent the next few hours checking each one. She had nearly given up but after telling herself *just one more* she found the box she was looking for.

This particular box was hidden right at the back, and unlike the others it wasn't so much a box but rather a wooden chest with a rusty old padlock holding it shut. She was a little worried at first that she wouldn't be able to open it but to her delight she found it wasn't locked and she opened it with ease. Inside were some dusty old candle sticks with several different coloured candles, metal bowls, photographs, jewellery, shiny coloured stones, and a bundle of clothes tied with a silk scarf, stuffed in amongst some even more unusual artefacts. She didn't want to waste any time examining them, so she quickly untied the bundle and found what she'd been looking for. Mum's Halloween costume.

Well, that is how she had remembered it. There was a jade green velvet cloak, matching pointed hat, and a broomstick. She tried them on, and they fitted her perfectly.

"Now I can go to the party," she sang loudly whilst dancing and twirling the broomstick, feeling proud of herself.

Later that day she had a text message from Charlie telling her the plan.

B at mine 4 9, number 13.

She had never been to his flat before despite passing it many times on her way to school. She found it strange that although *he* called her *Mystery,* she didn't know much about him either. But she did know that he had taken her under his wing and had looked out for her when he saw the other children tease her.

As predicted, her father came home from the pub and went straight to his bed. Misty waited until she heard him snoring and dressed herself in her mother's costume before heading to Charlie's. It was nine o clock and dark outside, the cloudless sky showed the moon, full and bright, shining down on her. She looked up and greeted it.

"Hello sister moon," she said, a phrase she had heard her mum say when the moon was full, something she had totally forgotten until now.

There was still lots of activity in the neighbourhood with children out late dressed up as monsters, witches, and skeletons swinging their pumpkin buckets filled with sweets. She saw older kids on their bikes shouting to each other, and rucksacks filled with eggs and toilet paper. The atmosphere seemed electric, and she got more excited with every step.

Before long she arrived at Charlie's address. He lived in a downstairs flat in the next block, number thirteen. *Yes, this was the right address* she told herself. However, there were no decorations or noise coming from the flat and she wondered whether he was playing a trick on her. What if there wasn't a party, what if he was watching and laughing at her right now?

She pushed those thoughts away and pressed the doorbell. She had butterflies in her stomach, and she felt her heart flutter. Misty wanted so much to have a nice time, but something just didn't seem right. A minute later the door opened, and a woman stood before her. She recognised her immediately.

"Welcome Misty, long time no see, come in." She said. So, afraid to refuse, wide eyed, and trembling, Misty went inside.

CHAPTER 10

"Aunt Bella?" Misty felt confused, *what was she doing here*?

"What's going on?" She asked, but her Aunt Bella said nothing. She was dressed in a long black gown with a hood half covering her face, but Misty knew it was her, she'd never forget her own aunt. She stepped over the doorstep as if she had no will of her own. She wanted to turn and run out of the door, but Aunt Bella was behind her now, and she heard the door slam shut.

With her legs trembling beneath her she continued down the narrow hallway and through to the living room. She knew Aunt Bella was following her as she could hear her breathing and felt the warmth from her breath on the back of her neck. Without any warning she felt a sharp tap on her shoulder and Misty tumbled through the open door, skidded to a stop, and landed quivering on the floor. Not wanting to see what was before her, she kept her eyes squeezed shut. When she finally opened them, she wished she hadn't.

The room was dimly lit and smelled horrible, like rotten apples and boiled cabbage.

The orangey glow of dying embers from the log burner picked up the shapes formed by a group of people sat in a circle on the floor. Misty couldn't see their faces as they too had hoods which reached right over their heads. None of them said a word, they just sat there like macabre mannequins, silent and motionless.

She wondered if this could be Charlie's idea of a scary party. Her thoughts swirled around trying to make some sort of sense of it all.

What if it was a lookalike, a nasty prank, and Charlie? Where was he?

"Charlie?" She whispered. *Where's Charlie?* She looked at the others but had no response. Misty turned and saw Aunt Bella; her face was contorted, and the grimace made Misty shudder. Aunt Bella's eyes were deathly black and shining like onyx. Her teeth were yellow and crooked, and looked like they could tear the flesh from any bone. Misty thought she was going to throw up, then Aunt Bella threw back her head and laughed the most terrible laugh Misty had ever heard. The deep throaty cackle echoed around the room and shook some plaster from the ceiling, Misty saw lumps of it fall and crumble as it bounced onto the hard, wooden floor.

As the bits of plaster fell around her, Misty thought she could hear voices coming from the next room. They started as a low mumble, then got louder and louder but she couldn't make out what they were saying. Two people entered the living room chanting words that made no sense to her. Her heartbeat even faster when she realised one of them was Charlie. He walked straight past her, followed by a woman, who given their resemblance Misty assumed was his mother. She thought for a moment that he would reassure her that this was all a big joke, she hoped he would wink and show her his big toothy smile, but no. Charlie was also dressed in the same black gown, but his hood was down revealing his face, and she noticed he was carrying a large metal pot. Whatever was in it was bubbling and it smelled horrible.

"Charlie?" Misty looked at him for an explanation or at least a response. "What's going on?" Charlie ignored her and carried on chanting. Misty wondered if he knew she was even there as he didn't acknowledge her. The fear she felt at this moment was like nothing she had ever experienced. Misty was terrified.

Charlie, still chanting, placed the steaming pot in the middle of the floor and sat down with the others who started chanting the same strange words, repeating them together over and over. The woman sat next to him, and the others took down their hoods. Misty scanned their faces quickly. She didn't recognise them but noticed they all had the same dead eyed expression; all of them were looking straight through her. Aunt Bella stood in the middle next to the pot, and with a spindly finger beckoned Misty to join her. Misty did as she commanded. She didn't feel she had a choice.

Then the chanting stopped. Aunt Bella smiled, her crooked teeth gleaming in the dim light, her arms raised like she was about to conduct an orchestra. Then, she spoke.

"Welcome," she said, removing her hood and gown, revealing a scarlet satin dress which clung to her bony body like cling film around a chicken wing. Then she lowered her arms and placed one hand on Misty's head. Despite her thin fragile frame, the weight of her hand was heavy, and Misty thought her neck might crack.

"We have gathered here on this special night to celebrate." Aunt Bella continued, "this night, when the veil between the worlds is at its thinnest."

Aunt Bella's voice was now so loud that Misty held her hands over her ears. She wanted to cry, but she held back her tears as she didn't want to show them how frightened she was.

"We are now ready to make our sacrifice, I will make the blood offering. Here stands my bloodline and her blood will ensure us safe passage." Aunt Bella was then handed a long ornate silver knife by Charlie, and she held the sharp edge to Misty's throat.

Misty froze, beads of sweat trickled down her forehead and she trembled with fear. She now knew for sure she was in real danger and had to do something, and quickly.

Up on the roof of the tower block there was a hub of dark energy emanating from Charlie's ground floor flat. Thick smelly darkness was seeping upwards, finding its way through each floor, twenty in all, until it eventually seeped through the top of the building, creating a green smoggy gloop that settled on the rooftop. Circling the rooftop, a woman on a broomstick was playing a flute, with a fat black cat sat on her lap. They circled around the green smoggy thick, but cloudless sky with the moon shining down on them. The woman was waiting.

In the ground floor flat, Aunt Bella, still holding the knife, instructed the group to chant again whilst she prepared herself for the sacrifice. Misty kept very still and came up with a plan to try and summon Wendy to her. Misty kept her eyes closed whilst trying to concentrate on Wendy's face in her mind's eye but, was all too aware of the cold metal of the knife against her neck. She sat like that for what felt like hours concentrating and trying not to faint with fear. She knew she had to bring her, otherwise she would be, well, she didn't want to think about it. Then something happened. Firstly, she thought she could hear whistling wind, then the sound of a flute and the tune she had come to know so well, then the windows rattled. *YES!* Misty had done it!

She suddenly she felt calm, in control and she instinctively knew what to do next.

Misty opened her eyes and looked around the room. She ignored the staring eyes, the bubbling cauldron and the knife now hovering close to her jugular. She noticed there was a clock on the wall, and she could just about make out the time. It was later than she expected, ten minutes past eleven. She closed her eyes again and concentrated on the seeing the second hand moving. Tick ... tick ... tick.

When she felt the time was right, Misty spoke the time.

"Eleven past eleven," she said quietly to herself. She opened her eyes and saw the second hand move off the number two. *Yes!* She thought and counted again.

Tick ... tick ... tick ... tick ... tick ... tick ... tick ... tick ... tick ... tick and tick.

"Eleven, eleven and eleven seconds," she said out loud, and as she did a gap suddenly appeared in front of her, a large gaping hole shimmering and pulsating within the room. She wasn't sure if anyone else saw the gap and she didn't care, it was big enough for her to fit through, and that is exactly what she was going to do. Before she could change her mind, Misty pushed Aunt Bella's hand out of her way, jumped up from the floor and flung herself through the hole. She didn't look behind, but if she had, she would have seen the gap closing behind her. Misty, could however, hear a loud screech that sounded like a wounded animal, which of course was Aunt Bella.

CHAPTER 11

Once inside the gap Misty noticed steps appear in front of her. They wound round and round, and up and up. Misty started climbing. As she climbed higher, she felt her breathing become tight and shallow. The air smelled stale and damp, and each step she took echoed in her ears. Just when she thought she couldn't keep going any longer she smelled the air becoming cleaner and fresher, and she saw an opening above her head. Using both hands and all her strength she pushed through the tiny door, which seemed to be held with a spring, and out she came onto the roof of the tower block. She could see a green smog rising from the roof, evaporating into the night air. She felt such relief that she had made it out, that she just lay there, stretching out on her back, breathing, smiling, and staring at the dark sky above her. Stars twinkled and the full moon shone brightly. Misty felt there was magic in the air.

"Hello again sister moon," she said, and could have sworn she heard the moon greet her back.

"Get up, quickly. Misty, get up."

Misty turned and saw Shadow's furry face looking down at her. His whiskers tickled her cheek and his green eyes sparkled. Misty was so pleased to see him that she reached out to touch his soft mane, but he wasn't having any of it and pulled away from her.

"No time for that," he said. "We need to go," and with that he leapt into the air.

Wendy, who was hovering near by, caught him in her lap and offered Misty her hand. Misty grabbed it and swung herself around and onto the back of the broomstick. She wrapped both arms around Wendy's waist and in a split second they were off.

"I expect you have many questions Misty, but first we must go somewhere safe." Wendy said in a firm but reassuring manner.

The speed at which they flew through the sky took Misty's breath away. She looked down at the lights of the city, which were getting further away now. She thought of her father, would he wonder where she was? She hoped he was still asleep and would be none the wiser when she returned home. But what if she didn't get to return home?

More questions than answers, she thought, so decided to put them to the back of her mind for now and just enjoy the moment. She squeezed Wendy's waist even tighter, held her head back and felt the breeze over her entire body. Misty laughed out loud with sheer bliss and Wendy joined in. Laughing together, she felt so close to Wendy, like she had known her for an eternity.

Misty looked down and saw they had left the city behind, all she could see now was the tops of trees and hills. Up ahead she saw mountains drawing closer and within seconds they were flying over them. Wendy rode her broomstick like it was a bird, guiding it swiftly over the mountain tops then swooping lower. The air was cold, and she felt it prickle her cheeks. She was starting to get earache but didn't care and embraced the icy coldness. The rest of her was warm like toast, her velvet cape and hat keeping her warmer than she would have expected.

Oh no the broomstick! She thought. She had left her mum's broomstick behind at Charlie's flat, she could kick herself for forgetting it, but given the urgency of her departure it was understandable.

"Here we are, brace yourself," said Wendy as she got ready to land.

She angled the broomstick downward and like the Big Dipper rollercoaster at Blackpool they plummeted to the ground. Misty's stomach flipped over, and she closed her eyes tightly, hanging on for dear life; she felt a bump, bump, and another bump until they stopped.

"You can open your eyes now," said Wendy and gently nudged her shoulder. Misty opened them and couldn't believe what she saw.

"So, this place is real?" She asked, seeing the same hill and stone circle she had seen in her dream.

"Of course, it's real Misty, you've been here already. Your dream wasn't a dream, well, it kind of was, you just arrived in a different way. I'll explain it all another time," said Wendy shaking off her black feathers that were now falling around her feet.

"Now you shake" she instructed.

Misty wiggled each leg and saw similar black feathers fall off her boots.

"What's with the feathers?" She really wanted to know.

"All in good time, now we must go and meet the others."

"Others?" She followed Wendy who was marching on ahead carrying her broomstick like it was a walking cane with Shadow trotting beside her.

Misty picked up her pace and caught up with them, they weren't far from the stones and before long they were entering the stone circle. She noticed that the moon was larger than she'd ever seen it, she could even see the craters, and it gave off a silver glow which made the stones seem even bigger and more magnificent than before. They seemed as tall as houses, and she felt tiny in comparison.

Misty went over to where Wendy was stood. She was looking up at the sky and muttering something about perfect timing. Then she got out her flute and started playing the same beautiful tune she always played. As she played, one by one, a crow appeared on each of the stones until there were eleven crows. They hopped to the ground, and she watched as they each transformed into their human form, shaking their feathers around their feet. Misty knew them all, she had met them in her dream, or well, whatever it was.

"What's the time Misty?" Asked Wendy.

"I don't know," she said shrugging her shoulders.

"Time is magic Misty, work it." Wendy said with a serious face.

Misty suddenly knew what Wendy meant, so she closed her eyes and raised her arms up toward the moon.

"It's eleven fifty-nine," she said with conviction. Wendy smiled.

"Then we have one minute until midnight," she said, and they all gathered together.

Dressed in their cloaks and hats with a peaceful moonlit glow upon their faces, they joined hands and formed a circle within the circle of stones, with Wendy in the centre.

Misty would never forget the peace she felt at the time, with these people, with Wendy and of course with Shadow, who was curled up on a stone snoozing. She swayed and hummed to the tune that Wendy was playing on her flute, enjoying the closeness of holding hands with these newfound friends.

"TIME?" Wendy asked.

Misty counted - *one, two, three* - in her mind and then shouted.

"MIDNIGHT!"

As she did, they all raised their arms up in the air, she felt a surge of energy pass between them, then a huge ball of white light appeared in the middle of the circle. It was moving and circling the group as if greeting each of them personally. The light was shimmering and fluttering, and then Misty saw it change. It seemed to burst, and before her stood the most beautiful woman she had ever seen. She couldn't begin to describe her, it was as though her beauty was coming from within her soul, and she felt like their souls were merging and for that moment she knew everything there was to know. The woman smiled at her and gently kissed her hand. Misty tingled all over, like a current of electricity was coursing through her veins. Then the woman whispered in her ear.

"The magic is within you." With that, she was gone.

Misty fell to her knees and looked around. Everyone was smiling and laughing, she got up and ran to Wendy who was smiling serenely. She looked deep into Misty's eyes and spoke.

"We did it Misty, you helped bring her to us, one of the most powerful beings we know, the Goddess of the moon."

Misty blinked and said nothing, she was overwhelmed.

"You are the missing piece of the puzzle we've all been waiting for; you don't yet know the power you have within you, but realise this Misty Morgan, you have much work to do." Wendy grinned.

Misty still said nothing, she had no words.

Misty couldn't remember getting home, she just found herself back on her pull out bed surrounded by black feathers and still wearing her cloak and hat. She sighed with relief that she was home safe, but she was also still a little terrified at almost being sacrificed by her villainous aunt. Everything was quiet but for the ticking of the grandfather clock in the hallway and the snoring from her father in the next room. She smiled to herself as she remembered the broomstick ride, meeting the others, and the Goddess! *She was so beautiful,* was her last thought as she tucked herself under the duvet. As her head touched the pillow, she was asleep.

CHAPTER 12

Misty rose early the next day. She had slept well considering the strange events of the day before. She had been a little worried about her father, and hoped he hadn't noticed her disappearance, but she needn't have concerned herself as he'd drunk enough beer and whiskey to sink a battleship and slept until midday.

Misty spent the morning writing in her Book of Shadows. She wrote down her spell using time. She understood now, that if she guessed the time as it happened then she could make the impossible happen, and that was *her* magic. But she wanted to know more, she needed to understand why all of this was happening to her. She also needed to know more about Aunt Bella and why she wanted to kill her, and Charlie. What was that all about?

I thought he was my friend. She thought, as she remembered him handing Aunt Bella the knife. Misty decided she would sit down with her father and see if he could shed some light on it all; she guessed he had not been completely honest with her, and probably for good reason.

Misty roused her father with the promise of lunch. She made a special effort and managed to rustle up two pretty good cheese omelettes, with plenty of ketchup, for them both. He complained that he had a headache, so she also brought him a jug of water and an aspirin. He smiled and told her he was grateful and that he didn't deserve such a good daughter, given his behaviour. Misty told him not to worry and that she loved him regardless, and so they ate their food sat on the sofa watching their broken television. The blank screen made them both sad, but they laughed nonetheless, and her father promised her he'd get a new one when he next got paid. She'd heard that many times before but pretended to be happy about it.

"Dad, will you tell me about Aunt Bella?" She asked, trying not to rouse any suspicion. "Do you ever hear from her?" She added as she cleared up their dirty dishes.

"Well, I don't know, I never saw much of her anyway, not since you were small. Your mother and her had a big falling out, I'm not even sure I know why. Hmm, maybe it was ... you know I really don't remember." Her father said, scratching his head.

He looked at her. "Why do you ask?"

Misty brushed it off and said she had found the old diary her aunt had given her one Christmas and was just wondering.

"Oh! I remember that diary, your mother had the same one, she used to write her spells ..." he stopped, looked at her and pondered for a moment. "Misty, there is something you should know, I wasn't sure if I would ever need to tell you, but I think you're now old enough to know. Your mother was ... is ... a witch."

He hesitated and looked at her, trying to judge her reaction. Misty gasped, now that did make sense.

"And Aunt Bella?" She asked.

"Yes, Bella too," he said shaking his head sadly. "But she, unlike your mother was poisonous, evil to the core."

Misty noticed that his eyes filled up and she thought he was going to cry, but he composed himself and went to the kitchen to get himself a beer and poured her a large glass of cola.

"Here you are." He handed her the glass, "I'll tell you what I remember."

"I met your mother in school, but you probably know that already. She was smartest girl in my year. She was popular and had lots of friends, all the boys wanted to date her and when she chose me, I felt the luckiest boy alive. We were both sixteen, I don't know what she saw in me, I wasn't as smart as her, but we got on really well. She was funny, and we used to laugh all the time. We would spend our time listening to music and going for walks in the woods. She taught me all about nature and I taught her to read music. We would write songs together, and she had the most beautiful singing voice, I was in awe of her." He stopped for a moment and smiled.

"Then, one day she took me back to her house and introduced me to her parents. It was then that I first met Bella. The house was a big old house in the country and ..." He stopped and looked distracted.

"What's wrong?" Misty asked.

"Oh, nothing darling, it's just I haven't thought about this in a long time ..." He paused.

"Anyway, I thought it a bit strange that I hadn't met her before. It turned out they were twins and I wondered why she wasn't in school. Your mother told me she was home schooled because of her behaviour, apparently, she had been expelled but she didn't tell me why. She was as pretty as your mother but there was something about her that made me uneasy. I think it was the way she looked at me, like she didn't want me around, like she was jealous or something. The long and short of it was she didn't like me, and I didn't like her either."

Misty listened intently. She remembered meeting Aunt Bella a few times as a child and hadn't been fond of her but didn't know why, it was just a feeling. Misty looked at her father and he seemed more troubled now, somehow lost in his thoughts. Then he continued.

"I found out they were witches when their parents died. Your gran and grandad were too, you see. There was lots of talk in the village at the time, mostly tittle tattle about them, and I'd heard rumours that Bella was responsible for their deaths. I didn't mind that your mother was a witch, she was such a good person and I loved her. I still do."

Misty had never asked about her grandparents. Mum didn't mention them, so she hadn't thought to ask.

"What happened to them?" She asked.

"Well, it was horrible, there was a fire, and Bella was in the house at the time. Your mother was with me, out on a date, and when we got home the house was already destroyed and Bella was nowhere to be seen. She was found days later wandering in the local woods. The police said it could have been arson as they found evidence of black witchcraft in Bella's bedroom. They couldn't prove it, but from then on Bella lived away, with a relative, I believe. Your mother came to live with me and your Nan and Grampa, my parents. They loved your mother too. I didn't see Bella again until you were born, she just turned up one day. I remember your mother wasn't happy about it but from then on Bella would just turn up from time to time, usually with gifts for you. Nothing for Michael, just you."

He looked sad and said, "your mother was a kind person, a powerful witch too. She had special gifts but never really used them to their full potential. I think Bella had something to do with that." He swigged his beer, stood up and looked out of the window, then he turned to Misty.

"Do you want to see your mother?"

Of course, she did, she hadn't seen her in five years and the last time was awful. Seeing her mum in hospital had broken her heart. Misty had heard the grown-ups say that she'd had a breakdown. She had no idea what that meant, but it didn't sound good. But now she felt ready, she missed her so much.

"Can we? And Michael?" She replied.

"Yes, I think it may be time, but I don't know about Michael," he said as he sat back in his chair taking another swig of beer. "I've heard that he's still with Bella, and I don't think he's coming back."

Her father sat back and closed his eyes. She decided not to ask anymore, that was enough for now and she hated seeing her father so sad.

"I'm going for a lie down," he said and went back to his bedrooam for a sleep.

Misty sat on her pull-out bed and thought about everything she had learnt over the past few days. It had been such a strange week and there was a lot of information for her to process.

She had found out she was a witch, as well as her mother, her aunt, her grandparents, her teacher, school nurse, dinner lady, all the others, and even Fragile Fiona. They were all witches. She had witnessed so many strange events and had almost been killed, had flown on a broomstick, travelled to a magical stone circle, and met the Moon Goddess. Then, there was Charlie.

Oh Charlie, my friend. Misty sighed. She thought of how he had betrayed her, which made her feel angry and sad at the same time. She needed a plan. She needed to get her mum's broomstick back and destroy whatever Aunt Bella was planning, because whatever it was it wasn't good.

CHAPTER 13

Now on a mission, Misty took her Book of Shadows and opened it to a fresh page. She had a feeling that she needed to work on a spell although she hadn't a clue where to start. Despite her lack of experience, she thought she'd give it a go on her own. After all she'd been told that the magic was within her. But firstly, she thought she would at least need a wand. She sighed; she didn't have one. But she did have a box downstairs in the basement that contained her mum's cloak, hat, and broomstick. *I wonder if she had a wand too?* She grabbed the key to the lock-up and headed downstairs.

It didn't take long for her to find her mum's wand. It was amongst all the other witchy looking things in the basement, and so she decided she would bring the wand, along with as much as she could carry back upstairs. Misty laid everything out on the kitchen table and examined the items one by one. She picked up the wand in her right hand and felt tingling shoot up her arm and out through the top of her head. Her mind went quiet, she had no thoughts, just feelings and the crystal attached to the tip started to glow. Instinctively, she used the crystal to rub the open page of her Book of

Shadows and before her eyes, words began to appear. Each word materialised until the page was filled, and it was then that the tingling stopped, and she could hear her thoughts again.

Meanwhile, back at Charlie's flat there was much activity. Bella had, with the help of the others, constructed a pyramid structure in the living room. It was made of willow sticks and held together with twine and a sticky herbal mixture. She had then placed a cauldron in the centre. Bella then instructed Charlie to find the ingredients for a spell intended for tonight. So, he headed down to China town with a list, a purse full of money and no idea why he was there.

Charlie had known Bella for a few years, since his mother had invited her into their home for a tarot reading. His mother had been reading fortunes for as long as he could remember, and he was used to seeing her use her tarot cards for anyone who would pay. Besides, she had needed extra money to make ends meet. He had wanted to believe there was something in it but hadn't been truly convinced, not until recently when he had seen Bella cast powerful money spells for them. Now Charlie was enjoying the best food around and they were planning a holiday to Florida, and so with the promise of more treats he gladly obeyed her orders.

Charlie wandered around the Chinese supermarkets with his list trying to read the labels that were written in Chinese. He had his phone translation App but was getting more than a little frustrated. However, he did manage to get what she had asked for and went home carrying a bag full of exotic ingredients, some of which needed to be treated "with caution" according to the shop keeper who had eyed him with suspicion.

When he arrived home the living room was lit with candles. The others were sat silently inside the pyramid dressed in black gowns, and his mother was helping Bella in the kitchen. She was dressed in a long black gown which was adorned with silver jewellery. Bella was wearing an extraordinary outfit, a flowing long black satin dress which rustled when she moved, and on her head was a huge black pointed hat with a dead magpie pinned to the rim. Her fingers were adorned with huge silver rings with stones in each, the colour of blood. She had a fur stole around her shoulders which looked like it was once a cat. Charlie winced when he noticed the lifeless head and paws hanging down around her shoulders. Bella's face seemed calm and emotionless, her eyes were black, and her mouth was painted with scarlet lipstick. His mother smiled at him.

"Well done son, you've made me proud," she said as she took the bag from his quivering hand. "Now go and get changed and sit with the others."

Charlie did as he was told.

Whilst Charlie was getting ready, Misty was already prepared and feeling quietly confident. The Book of Shadows had provided her with the spell, now all she had to do was, do it.

She cleared the table and carefully put the witchy things safe under her pillow, apart from the wand and an old pocket watch that she found with her mum's things, she would need those for her spell. Next, she put on her mum's jade green cloak and pointed hat, checked on her father who was still sound asleep, and with her wand safely in her pocket she left the flat. She had considered calling Wendy for back up but for some reason she thought she might already be watching over her. Besides, she wanted to do this herself.

Misty walked slowly and silently towards Charlie's home whilst concentrating on her breathing, counting each one, in, and out. With each breath and step she took she felt more confident. Misty's intent was clear in her mind, she knew exactly what she wanted and nobody, not even Bella would stop her. So, with her mum's broomstick clearly in her mind's eye she knocked the door three times.

With her heart booming in her chest and with her wand in her right hand she recited the spell to herself and waited for the door to open.

Then she saw a light go on in the hall and she almost lost her nerve and fled. However, she remained determined, stood her ground, and took a deep breath in. The door opened and before her stood Charlie's mother. She was dressed in a black gown and had a big toothy smile, just like Charlie's.

"Misty Morgan, you came back. You must come in child; we've been waiting for you." She said and ushered her through the door. She checked outside to see if Misty had brought company, and satisfied she was alone, she slammed the door shut and led her through to the living room.

CHAPTER 14

Although Misty had prepared her spell, she quite hadn't prepared herself for what was to come. She braced herself and entered the living room. The nasty smell of rotting apples and boiled cabbage hit her, making her retch, and with the dim light she couldn't quite make out what was going on. As her eyes adjusted to the darkness, she could see what looked like a pyramid in the centre of the room. She gasped when she saw the construction made of twigs and twine and so tall it reached the ceiling. There was noxious green smoke seeping from between the gaps that made it look as though it was burning. The smoke hit the back of her throat causing her to choke, and she spluttered whilst trying to catch her breath. Charlie's mother took her by the arm and led her to the entrance of the sinister structure. As she approached, she heard sounds coming from within it, like a low hum resonating which as she got closer made her body gently vibrate.

Charlie's mother beckoned her to go inside, Misty hesitated, feeling fearful of what might be there and the memory of that knife against her throat still vivid in her mind. However, now armed with a newfound courage, and her spell, she ducked her head and went through the small entrance.

When she looked up, she saw a group of people sat in a circle, all dressed in the same hooded gowns. She sat down in the only space available and looked around at their faces, finding Charlie was amongst them. He looked up at her and glared. His eyes were menacing, and he was no longer the cheerful toothy grinned boy she'd grown to admire. Then he lowered his head and continued to hum.

Misty looked to her left side and noticed the person was nervously wringing their hands. She could just see under the hood and immediately recognised the sticky out ears and cleft chin of her brother. Her stomach flipped.

"Michael?" She whispered, so only he could hear. "Is that you?"

He didn't reply and continued to hum with the others.

The humming was making Misty's head throb and she felt sick. Her skin was itchy like ants were crawling over her, and her thoughts were confused. Out of the corner of her eye something glistened. Charlie was holding the same silver knife that had been placed against her neck. He sniggered when he knew she had seen it and then put it back beneath his gown. For a moment she'd forgotten why she was there and thought maybe she was having a bad dream. Now all she was wanted was to get out of there and take Michael with her, but she was trapped. Somewhat distracted by what she was witnessing, she tried to remember why she was there, but her mind was foggy, and her senses were dimming. She put her hand inside her pocket and felt her wand. It felt warm and comforting and her mind cleared a little.

The spell, I must remember the spell, she thought, and then she put her hand in the other pocket and felt around. She could feel the ticking of the pocket watch.

Yes, I remember ...

Misty wasn't sure how much time had passed before Aunt Bella appeared. She crawled headfirst through the entrance, first taking off her grotesque, dead magpie hat as there wasn't enough room for it, then sat in the middle, carefully placing the hat back on her head. Bella was a formidable presence within that small space, and she seemed to exude such vileness that she immediately commanded everyone's attention. They all sat up straight and looked at her.

"At last, we have all been brought together." Bella said fervently, "now we can begin. Michael we'll start with you," and she tapped Michael on his head with a long claw-like fingernail.

He looked up. Misty could see his eyes now, they seemed empty, emotionless, and he didn't acknowledge her. Misty nudged him with her elbow to see if he would react, but still nothing. She wondered if Aunt Bella had bewitched him. Her mouth was dry with fear and the thought of Michael being taken from her was enough to make her boil with rage. She was now more determined than ever to take back her broomstick and maybe if she had enough power, her brother too.

Misty put her hand back in her pocket and again felt around for her pocket watch. She smoothed it with her fingers and brought it out for a moment to check the time, five minutes to midnight. She had learned to change the time with the little metal wheel on the side and had practiced earlier, she knew exactly how it worked and felt comfort knowing it was there, quietly ticking in time with her heartbeat. All she had to do now was remember her spell, word for word.

As Misty prepared to cast her spell Michael started to speak. She realised immediately that he was invoking something bad, the tone of his voice was raspy and deep, and he spoke of things she didn't understand, nor did she want to. Then he started to retch, louder and louder as if bringing up phlegm. Misty hesitated for a moment but was determined to stay focused so ignored the green froth now coming from his mouth. Holding the watch in her left hand, she took out the wand from her pocket, pointed it at Aunt Bella and cast her spell. She spoke the words as though they flowed through her veins, and they seemed to grow in strength as she uttered them with such command that she surprised herself.

"May evil deeds be wiped out
And good take their stead
The spell I intone
Shall see thee undone
By flesh and by bone
By sea and by sky
By sun and by moon."

Misty put down her wand and quickly turned the wheel on the watch until the time went back by twenty-four hours and continued.

"There you stay until you pay
May wisdom grow
Till good you show
Bring me my broom
Or be there doom!"

Misty turned the little wheel back to the current time. It was now midnight. She picked up her wand and just as a bolt of electricity turns on a lightbulb, her wand lit up and everyone within that pyramid appeared to freeze. They remained motionless, suspended in time and powerless to stop her.

Misty could see Aunt Bella with her contorted face, unblinking and with a grimace so terrible that she had to look away. She clambered over the others, who were now resembling macabre waxwork statues of themselves, and left the pyramid.

Seeing her mum's broomstick leaning against the far wall, Misty grabbed it. She thought for a moment she should go back for Michael but decided against it, as she wasn't sure how long the spell would hold and didn't want to take that risk, at least not for now. She decided she would leave and consult with Wendy before coming up with a plan to rescue Michael. With her wand in her right hand, she straddled the broomstick, and as she did it seemed to come alive. She could feel it pulsating beneath her; it was as though it was breathing, and she felt their energies merge together until they were as one being. A surge of energy rose from beneath her and with a nudge of her knee she was away, the doors opening in front of her as she flew up into the cold night sky.

CHAPTER 15

The moment that Misty sat on her broomstick everything changed. Her senses heightened and her fear diminished. She had merged with it, and she felt they were now connected forever. She marvelled at the world around her, everything looked so different, more colourful, sharper, and brighter. With the city beneath her Misty looked down over the roof tops. She saw twinkling lights and chimney smoke rising into the night sky; she went higher and higher until, they disappeared from view. Looking up she witnessed a shooting star. She thought she should make a wish, but she didn't need to as she could already make her wishes come true. She was as free as a bird, riding the wind and with just the moonlight to guide her she headed back home.

Meanwhile back at Charlie's flat, the spell had already worn off.

"Get up you spineless fools," Bella screeched.

Her coven of witches were looking at each other bewildered and confused, scrabbling around on the floor, and knocking into each other trying to get out of the pyramid. Bella barged her way out not caring that she broke the structure, leaving willow twigs and twine collapsing on top of them. She grabbed her broomstick and jumped on. The witches didn't see her leave as she vanished in an instant. Bella had been using a broomstick since she was a child and was able to expertly manoeuvre it. She jetted past the tower blocks and headed in the direction of Misty. She could smell her scent, and like a bloodhound she followed it.

Michael remained cross legged on the floor, staring straight ahead, still unable to gather his thoughts. The other witches were busy untangling the willow and untying the twine until the pyramid was just a big pile of twigs in the corner of the room. They ignored Michael, who remained there, bewildered until he was eventually roused by Charlie.

"Michael, Michael." He said whilst poking his ribs, "get up, your sister has gone. She's got her broomstick and she's left. Bella has gone after her," he yelled.

Michael blinked and his eyes were no longer vacant. He looked Charlie in the eyes. "We've made a terrible mistake," Michael said, "Bella will destroy her, we've got to do something."

Then Michael pushed Charlie out of the way and headed to the front door. When he opened it, a large gust of wind hit him in the face. He went to step out, but the wind held him back. He pushed himself forward until he was face to face with an old woman wearing a purple pointed hat. It was Wendy who was stood in front of him with one hand on her hip, and the other holding her broomstick.

"Get on," she said, and without hesitation Michael did so, and with his arms wrapped tightly around her waist they headed off into the sky.

With home within her sight, Misty slowed down and got ready to land, but she heard something closing in behind her and turned to look. She saw Aunt Bella just a few metres away and heading straight for her. Misty could see the crazed look on her aunt's face and the magpie on her hat now seemed to be alive, flapping its wings and squawking loudly.

"Stupid girl, you won't get away that easy." Bella screamed and launched herself directly at her.

Misty had now landed outside the door to the main building, her home was nearly in reach, and she rummaged quickly for her key. She found it and within a second or two she was through the door, slamming it shut and leaving Bella behind with her nose pressed against the glass window. Misty's heart was racing, and she was shaking from head to toe. But she was safe, for now. Carrying her broomstick, she ran quickly up the stairs until she reached her flat door only to be met by Shadow who was sitting proudly on the doorstep.

"Hello Misty, you took your time," he said as she opened the door and he trotted in behind her.

Misty's heart was still beating fast, and her ears were aching from the cold wind. She smiled to herself as she breathed in the musty smell of the gloomy flat. For the first time since moving there she felt relieved to be home.

Everything was in darkness and the flat was quiet except for the ticking of the grandfather clock and her father's snoring bellowing out from his bedroom. Misty tiptoed past his door and into the living room. She turned on the lamp, pulled out her bed as quietly as she could. She gently placed her broomstick under the bed, then took off her mother's cloak and hat and hid them under a cushion. Finally, she crept into the kitchen, poured herself a large glass of milk and helped herself to biscuits before returning to her makeshift bedroom. Shadow was already curled up on her bed.

"Do you want some milk?" She whispered to him with a mouth full of jammy dodger, "or some cheese? I'm afraid we don't have much here," she said making a face.

Shadow looked up at her and yawned.

"I've just eaten," he said and closed his eyes.

Misty finished her milk and biscuits, flopped on the bed, and snuggled in next to Shadow. He smelled of the outdoors and his soft fur tickled her cheeks. She closed her eyes and snuggled in closer. She could feel the vibration of his purring, which made her feel calm and a few minutes later she was fast asleep.

While Misty slept peacefully a wild wind was raging outside. Wendy had spotted Bella pursuing Misty so had decided to take up the chase. Wendy could feel Michaels's heart pounding as he squeezed her waist tightly, so she looked around for a safe place to hide him. She spotted the ideal place and brought her broomstick down to land in a nearby garden.

"Stay hidden and stay safe," Wendy whispered to Michael as she carefully opened someone's garden shed. "I'll be back in two flicks of a cat's tail."

Satisfied that Michael would be safe, Wendy skilfully mounted her broomstick and soared back into the midnight sky.

Frightened and lonely, Michael shivered with the cold and wondered what would become of him. He had been a prisoner for so long now that he had no idea how to survive in this world. All he had were his pack of playing cards which he took from his pocket. He shuffled them, picked out nine cards and laid them out in front of him. He would listen to the cards, and they would help him figure out what to do next.

Meanwhile, Wendy had caught up with Bella. The wild wind had now become a storm and rain was beating down on the two witches.

With sodden cloaks and hats they clashed their broomsticks together whilst they fought high above the ground. They both uttered incantations as the thunder boomed loudly above them, and flashes of lightening lit up the dark sky. Then a bolt of lightning came close to striking them both, causing them to tumble from the sky. They hit the ground, landing only metres from each other, and they both scrambled to their feet quickly to catch their broomsticks.

Wendy's broomstick narrowly missed her head, but she caught it gracefully in her right hand. Bella's broomstick, however, landed in front of an oncoming car and before she could reach it, the car hit it, breaking it into pieces. The wind scattered the pieces in different directions across the road. Bella looked on in horror. The driver stopped the car and got out. He picked up a piece of the broomstick and looked around to see if it belonged to anyone. He saw nothing but bits of wood being tossed around in the wind. So, he threw it to one side and drove off. He hadn't noticed Bella hiding behind a post box with a face that could curdle milk.

When Bella realised her broomstick was totally destroyed, she let out an almighty roar, which echoed around the neighbourhood.

"This isn't the end; I *will* get my revenge!" she screamed. Bella, defeated, soaking wet and without transportation trudged back to

Charlie's flat. Wendy looked on and chuckled to herself. She knew that the fight wasn't over, but things would be safe for a short while. She sniffed the air, hopped back on her broomstick and leaving a trail of black feathers behind, went to fetch Michael.

On returning to the shed, Wendy found Michael fast asleep on an old sun lounger. Spread out in front of him were nine playing cards. She looked at them and smiled. She knew the magic of the cards and saw, that although Michael didn't realise it yet, he also had magic within him. It was at that moment that she realised that Michael had a special part to play in how things were to turn out.

"You don't know it yet Michael, but your destiny has been shown to me." Wendy whispered. Michael stirred but didn't wake.

Wendy looked around and found herself a folding chair. She set it next to Michael, made herself comfortable and closed her eyes.

CHAPTER 16

The next morning Misty was woken by her father clattering around in the kitchen. He told her to get up as she was late for school. She sat up and the first thing she thought of was Shadow. She checked around the bed and there was a warm patch next to her pillow and a few black strands of fur, but he was nowhere to be seen.

"Ah puss, where are you?" She said out loud.

"What's that?" Asked her father, thinking she was talking to him.

She smiled to herself and changed the subject.

"I was thinking, I would like to see Mum soon, do you think that's possible?" She asked hopefully.

I guessed you would, so I've already made some arrangements," he said as he carried in a tray of buttered toast and orange juice.

This was the first time in ages that he had made her breakfast and she ate it heartily. Misty was overjoyed at the prospect of seeing her mum again, she just hoped that her father wasn't just stringing her along. Once she had eaten, she checked to see if her mum's cloak, hat, and broomstick were still hidden from view, which they were, and made her way to school.

It was raining outside which made the journey to school a little unpleasant. Misty was also worried about seeing Charlie. She wondered what she would say to him and kept replaying the events of yesterday over in her mind. It made her feel sad to think her friend had betrayed her, and worse still, been involved in such hateful activities. Misty wondered if he had just pretended to be her friend in order to lure her there in the first place. It all felt too much for her to cope with right now so decided she would just ignore him. Besides, she didn't want any more trouble from Aunt Bella. Misty's thoughts wandered to Michael. She was very upset to see him there, particularly as he seemed so much under the influence of Aunt Bella. She really needed to speak to Wendy today and come up with a plan to rescue him.

Misty's first lesson was Biology and Miss Grim seemed in a pleasant mood for a change. She smiled at the class and told them that today they would be dissecting rats. Miss Grim looked at Misty and told her to bring one out for each pupil.

"You know where to go," she said and pointed at the storeroom door.

Misty did as she was told and went into the storeroom, but she felt sad about having to do this especially after she had got to like the rats a little. She noticed that the cages where the rats had been last week were now empty and there was a pile of little lifeless bodies lined up on the slab in front of her. She sighed, and her heart felt heavy. Misty remembered the last time she was in this room with Wendy, the fun she had, and how much she wished she could see her again.

"Wendy," she said, "Wendy, Wendy, I need you."

The windows rattled, and Misty heard the familiar sound of the flute. She felt a flutter of wind, like someone's breath on her cheeks, and from behind the curtain Wendy appeared.

"Hello again, I was hoping you'd call me," said Wendy with a beaming smile. Then she looked down at the row of dead rats and sighed.

"There is so much to do and so many places to be. But first we will need to sort this out. Follow my lead," she said and pulled out her wand and a pocket watch from her pocket. She held the wand in her right hand and gave the watch to Misty.

"Now do your spell, like you did before," she instructed. Then Wendy muttered some words and pointed her wand at each rat whilst Misty used the little wheel on the side of the watch to turn back the time.

Wendy continued to mutter words that Misty didn't understand, as she tapped each rat with her wand. As she did so, they started to twitch and wriggle, then they opened their eyes and sniffed the air. Before long, all thirteen rats were sitting on the rim of Wendy's hat as right as rain.

"Now, go and tell Miss Grim there are no rats," said Wendy, looking just a little smug, "and I will meet you after school."

With that she was gone, and so were the rats. All that was left was a little pile of black feathers beneath the curtains.

A perplexed Miss Grim hunted high and low for the rats and couldn't understand what could have happened. She could have sworn she had them ready for dissection this morning.

After class Misty headed to the break room. Charlie was sat on the large comfy sofa eating a muffin and chatting with some friends. He looked up when he saw Misty walk in and made an excuse to go over and talk to her.

"Hey Mystery, not such a mystery now, are you?" He said with a grin, but his eyes weren't smiling. "Where's Michael?" He asked, as if she knew he was missing.

She said nothing, turned around and walked back out, sticking to her plan, and determined she wouldn't let him get to her.

But why would he ask me where Michael is? She wondered.

At lunchtime Misty was starving. She joined the long queue and when it was her turn for helpings she looked and saw Kitty Bloom, her favourite dinner lady serving the puddings. Her heart skipped a beat as she remembered their time together. She remembered the way she saw Kitty dance, light as air under the moonlight. Now she was just a plump old lady serving lunch. Kitty caught her eye and smiled, then she gave her a double helping of chocolate chip cake and custard.

"See you later." Kitty whispered.

Misty ate her pudding and with each mouthful wondered where the meeting would be. She really hoped it would be at the stones.

The last lesson of the day was History, and Misty had been excited to see Mr Woolley again since discovering that he was a witch too. She walked into class and saw him sat at his desk sorting papers. He looked up and winked at her. Misty's stomach flipped as she remembered seeing him shapeshift back from being a crow, and how they all danced and sang together. She also remembered how his face lit up when he greeted the Moon Goddess.

At the end of the lesson Mr Woolley went around the class handing out homework. When he came to Misty, he bent down and whispered in her ear.

"See you later," he smiled. Misty knew then that something wonderful was going to happen again.

On her way to the school gates, Misty wondered where she would meet Wendy as she had told Misty she would see her after school. She supposed that she would appear somewhere unexpectedly. As she was pondering this, she noticed Nurse Allgood talking with Fiona Le Fey by the gate, and they both looked up when they saw her coming. They looked as if they were waiting for her. Misty decided that this must be part of Wendy's plan and approached them.

"We're waiting for the bus Misty; do you want to join us?" Asked Fiona.

"Where are we going? I don't have my things with me," said Misty, thinking she would need her mum's cloak, hat and broomstick.

"Don't worry about that dear, you won't be needing those," said Nurse Allgood as if she had read her mind. "Just follow us."

Misty followed Nurse Allgood and Fiona to the bus stop and on their way, they were joined by Mr Woolley and Kitty Bloom, who both acknowledged Misty with a nod. Then Sami Singh, dressed in his Postman uniform, also joined them. He was followed by Eli the biker wearing his crash helmet, and then Ariana White who was carrying some dusty old books. After a few minutes, Mrs Murphy arrived with a big bag of sherbet lemons and handed them to Misty. Then Jabir the barber, who was laughing hysterically to himself at a joke he had just told his last customer, joined the group. Last to arrive was Myla McDuff. She seemed to glide toward them, pirouetted to a stop, curtsied, and then blew everyone a kiss. They all seemed so happy to see each other, and Misty was overjoyed to be in their company again, and in such normal surroundings too.

They must have waited there about ten minutes when the bus pulled in. It was empty, and they all piled on one by one. The driver winked at Misty as she boarded, and she recognised him as Rudy. He grinned.

"All aboard, brace yourselves we're in for a bumpy ride," he said, changing the destination on the front of the bus to read *NOT IN USE* and off they went.

Misty thought they might use a spell to transport them to wherever it was they were going, but it seemed they were taking a more traditional route. She sat happily on the seat next to Fiona who was quietly humming a tune to herself.

"Where are we going?" She asked her.

"To the stones," she replied with a smile, pausing her humming.

"Brilliant." Said Misty and gently squeezed Fiona's hand. "Where is Wendy?" She asked. Fiona stopped smiling and looked serious.

"Nobody knows. But don't worry, she's always on time when she really needs to be." Fiona replied. Then she gave a reassuring smile, closed her eyes, and returned to humming.

CHAPTER 17

Within a few minutes Fiona was sound asleep. Misty had so many questions that she wanted answers to. So, she turned to see who was on the bus 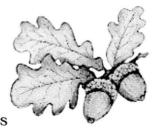 that might be able to shed some light on things. She guessed that all of them would have something to share. However, she left her seat and made her way to the back of the bus to sit next to Mrs Murphy. She guessed that given her age she might have the most to tell her.

Mrs Murphy budged up to allow room for Misty to sit comfortably and patted the seat with her hand.

"How 'ya Misty, c 'mere to me." She said in her soft sing-song Irish brogue.

"Hello Mrs Murphy, thank you for the sweets." Misty said politely. For the first time, she noticed that Mrs Murphy looked younger than she'd previously thought, her face only had a few wrinkles, her eyes sparkled, and she seemed to radiate a youthful glow.

Misty had so many questions that she didn't know where to start, so she sat silently for a few minutes trying to work out the most important question to ask. She was just about to speak when Mrs Murphy jumped in.

Why don't I tell you from the beginning?" She suggested and Misty nodded in agreement, so she began.

"Donkeys years ago, I'm not sure how many, four, or maybe even five hundred, there was a girl named Gwendolyn. She was born to a family who were so poor that they didn't even have a pot to pee in, so she was given away to a rich family who didn't have a child, and they raised her as their own.

As she grew older, she showed signs that she had magic in her bones, an unnatural power if you like. She would chatter with the animals and birds and could even control the wind and bring rain when it was dry. One day Gwendolyn, who was still a wean, maybe your age, was seen by a neighbour as she brought rain clouds to the fields. The crops were failing with drought and Gwendolyn thought to help the local farmer. But in those days Misty, people were fearful of things they didn't understand and thought her possessed by the devil and so they wanted her dead."

Mrs Murphy paused for a moment and took a sip of her herbal tea that she had in a small flask. She offered some to Misty who took a sip to be polite. She thought it tasted like pond water, so she sucked a lemon sherbet to get rid of the taste. But Mrs Murphy had another sip and continued.

"Anyhow, Gwendolyn was so frightened for her life that she ran away from home. She was found by an old woman who lived in the woods, who took her in and cared for her. It turned out the old woman was a healer who knew which plants and herbs to use to make people well. She knew about the seasons, the phases of the moon, all about the balance of light and dark, and about being in harmony with all nature: the plants, the trees and the creatures of the earth, sea, and sky. But this old woman was feared by the people too. They called her a witch. Back then witches were seen as devils, and they could be killed in the most terrible ways. This old woman knew that Gwendolyn was also a natural witch, and so she taught her all she knew. She helped her to control her powers, but her abilities grew stronger and stronger. Her power was such, that the old woman got scared that she would be caught and killed. So, they practiced a way to purposely shift their human forms into that of crows, in order to hide from the people who hunted them."

Mrs Murphy took another long sip of tea. Misty wondered where this story was going and who was she talking about, surely there must be some connection. She popped another lemon sherbet in her mouth and continued to listen.

"So, one day the old woman was caught by a mob of angry people, they wanted to blame her for a plague that had caused many deaths in their village. They believed she had used witchcraft against them all. They killed her

112

horribly and Gwendolyn saw what had happened and grew so angry and scared that she turned herself into a crow and flew far away. She spent a long, long time as a crow. She ate dead animals for food and slept high in the trees, and eventually, over time she forgot she was once a wean.

However, one day she was sat on a fence, and she heard someone play a beautiful tune on a flute. She remembered the music the old woman would play on her pipes, and this made her remember. So, she turned herself back into a human, but found that many years had gone by, almost a century. And yet she was still young like the wean she once was. The world was very different, and she had to learn new ways, so as to live in the world of people and also still be herself; she would spend her time as both human and crow. She survived this way and used her abilities to help those around her. So, Misty, what do you think was happening to Gwendolyn when she became a crow?" Misty scratched her head.

"Did time stay still or speed up? She replied, having a guess.

"Good answer Misty, well it would appear, that when she became a crow she entered into a different realm of the world, the *Otherworld*. It's hard to explain but, it's like when you dream, a bit like that vivid dream you had when we first met at the stones. She was in between the real world, like we are in now, and the dream world, where time is altered, either by going fast and slow, or backwards and forwards. So, you see, Gwendolyn learned to jump into this in-between world at will. Not many people are able to do this, and it's not without danger too, many people have got stuck there." Mrs Murphy looked at Misty and smiled.

"So, do you know *who* I'm talking about?" She asked. The penny had dropped now.

"So, Wendy's real name is Gwendolyn? Like, is she hundreds of years old?" Misty asked. Mrs Murphy looked at her with wide eyes.

"You know the oak tree in your garden, the old one you would climb, the one you called Jack?" Misty nodded vigorously.

Yes, his name was Jack. How does she know that? She wondered, excited that she knew his name at last.

"Well, Wendy grew that same tree from an acorn, yes that tree was in the same woods where she lived with that old woman. She named that special oak tree Jack, and so did you," said Mrs Murphy nodding and smiling.

She laughed at Misty who was so shocked she almost fell off her seat.

"Careful you don't choke on that sweet Misty," she said and had another sip of tea.

"So now you know, Wendy is a very special woman. A powerful, caring, and wise witch who has guided many of us over many hundreds of years, and now it is our turn to help her. You have also been chosen. These are special times Misty, she gathered us for a reason, all thirteen of us. Something terrible was unleashed forty years ago, and the time is now right for it to be destroyed," said Mrs Murphy with a serious look. She was no longer smiling and grabbed Misty by the hand and squeezed.

"We must all be very strong now and we will conquer this evil, together," she said, then let go of her hand. Misty felt uneasy, like she didn't know the full story, and that scared her. She still had many questions, not least about her brother, Aunt Bella, Charlie, and Shadow. Yes Shadow.

"Mrs Murphy? What about Shadow? Is he really a cat?" She asked.

"He's Wendy's familiar. Her assistant if you like. But, sure as eggs, he's a cat. Now, that's enough for now, I'm knackered and need a nap," and with that Mrs Murphy nodded off.

Misty looked around the bus and noticed that everyone apart from Rudy was asleep. She suddenly felt tired too, and with the motion of the bus she felt her eyes droop. Soon she was asleep with them.

CHAPTER 18

 Misty's father was getting worried now, it wasn't like her, she would always let him know if she would be home late. He looked at the grandfather clock in the hall. It had stopped. He needed to get that fixed, he thought. He checked his phone. It was nearly seven, so decided to leave it until eight before he started making phone calls. As he put his phone away, there was a knock on the door. Thinking maybe she had forgotten her key, he raced to answer it.

"Misty?" He said as he opened the door, but there before him, bedraggled and forlorn stood Michael, his son.

Neither of them said a word, they just looked at each other, trying to take each other in.

"Hi Dad," Michael said, before collapsing in a heap on the doorstep.

Robert couldn't quite believe his eyes. He held Michael in his arms for a moment before scooping him up and carrying him into the living room. Misty's bed was already pulled out, so he lay him down and went to close the front door. When he returned Michael was sat up looking at him, his eyes were red and his face

116

and hands were black with dirt, as were his clothes.

"Look at you," Robert said, not really knowing how to react. "You need a bath and a hot meal. I'll sort it out and then you can tell me all about it." He left him there to run the bath, and Michael, for the first time in five years, finally felt safe.

Outside on the window ledge sat a crow. She peered through the gap of the curtains and could see Michael laying on the bed. She watched as Robert came in with a plate of food and a mug of something hot. Satisfied, she stretched out her wings and flew off in the direction of the stone circle.

Across the street there was a black cat sitting on a different window ledge, peering through a small gap of another window, watching. What he saw made his fur stand on end. He arched his back and jumped down. Looking up, saw the crow. The crow looked down and they locked eyes, and as the crow continued to the stones, the cat sauntered off to a warm spot by the basement boiler room.

What Shadow had seen going on through the window had scared even him, a cat who was used to all sorts of peculiar happenings. He saw that Bella had confined all her witches to the living room, including Charlie, and they were engaged in a spell so hideous he couldn't watch. Bella was so full of rage that her face resembled that of a gargoyle. The others had no expression at all and appeared to be completely under her control.

Fifty miles or so away, in a privately-run hospital sat a woman. She had been there for five years and had barely spoken or left her room in that time. She was unrecognisable from the woman she once was. She was naturally small in stature and frame but now her bones protruded through her thin grey skin. Her eyes had sunk into their sockets and her hair was long and unkempt. She was reading a letter, the first one she had received since being there. She finished reading it and then, dressed only in her nightdress and slippers, she left the room. It was dark outside, but she made her way down the cold corridors toward the garden room and found a seat by the window and looked out. She looked up at the moon that was starting to wane. Its light glistened over the trees in the hospital grounds and like a switch going on in her mind, her memories started to flood back. She read the letter again and smiled.

A nurse saw the woman and approached her.

"Celeste? Is that you? What are you doing here?" She asked.

Celeste looked up and said, "My family are coming, isn't that wonderful?"

The nurse frowned, "I think you must be mistaken. Your family are dead, you know that."

She leant down to take her by the arm, but Celeste resisted.

"Liar," she said to the nurse, "Read that," and pointed to the letter.

The nurse glanced at the letter and could see it was from Celeste's husband Robert.

"I'll go and see the nurse in charge," she said and hurried away.

The nurse in charge was sat behind his desk reading a newspaper. He looked up over his glasses to see his most trusted nurse Mary stood in front of him panting.

"We have a problem Emrick," she said.

"Slow down Mary, what's up?" Said Emrick looking intrigued.

"It's Celeste, she knows her family are alive. I think you need to warn, *you know who*," she said, wide-eyed and terrified and afraid to say the name.

"Hmm, leave it with me. Go and see to Celeste and make sure she has her medication," he said.

Mary nodded and left, and Emrick went to his private locker room to change. He returned to his office wearing a long black hooded robe and carrying an old metal box in his hands. He locked the door behind him and taking the magical tools from his box he set up his alter on his desk.

At the same time, Wendy, who was fast approaching the stone circle, sensed something in the air. She looked up at the moon and whispered.

"Celeste?"

Wendy stopped, changed course, and flew as quickly as possible in the direction of the hospital.

Mary was now making her way back to Celeste, who was still sat in the garden room. Mary had with her a little plastic cup with tablets in it. When she arrived, Celeste was gazing out of the window at the moon, muttering something under her breath. She stopped when she saw Mary coming, and pretended she was reading her letter again.

"These are for you Celeste, it's important you take your medication," said Mary, "Now hold out your hand."

Celeste looked at the tablets and knew something was wrong. She didn't need medicine, all she needed to do now was trust her instincts. So, she took the plastic cup, thanked her politely and then pretended to take them, but really, she had them under her tongue, ready to spit out when Mary's back was turned. Reassured that she had taken her sedatives, Mary left her and went back to seeing to the other patients.

As soon as Mary was out of sight Celeste spat the tablets into her hand and threw them out of the window. She looked up at the moon and whispered.

"Thank you, sister," before sitting back down in the chair. She thought she heard something, like whistling coming from outside. She got up and pressed her face against the glass to see what it could be. She saw nothing, but the whistling grew louder, like music sweeping through the trees outside. The window rattled and a gust of wind blew it open, knocking Celeste backwards but she didn't fall or even stumble.

The wind. Yes, I know. She thought, and after five long years, Celeste woke up.

CHAPTER 19

Emrick was the Nurse in Charge and had worked at the hospital for the past five years. He couldn't remember applying for the job, but he remembered getting a letter addressed to him telling him to attend at *so and so* time and on *so and so* day. He just found himself at the hospital at the correct time with his best suit on with all his answers prepared, but with no idea what he was prepared for.

He later found out that the private hospital was once a Manor House owned by generations of wealthy landowners. However, the most recent owners died in peculiar circumstances which roused suspicion among the locals, especially as within a few weeks of them dying, a new owner appeared with big plans for a state-of-the-art mental health hospital. This mysterious new owner was a woman, and she appeared to be very rich with an ominous presence that Emrick found fascinating. She had interviewed him for the job but already seemed to know everything about him, which included his interest in magic. Her name was Bella.

Having spent most of his working life in charge of an inner-city hospital, Emrick was used to dealing with problems. In fact, he prided himself in his ability to handle life's "misfits" who were often in the midst of a crisis. Bella had enticed him with new challenges that only he could manage, for that's what she told him. She would often have a favour to ask of him with the promise of a reward of some kind, so he would always deliver, regardless of how bizarre or questionable it seemed. Every now and then she would turn up asking him questions, and always had a special interest in a patient named Celeste, but he never questioned why.

Five years later he was running the place like a well-oiled machine, or so he liked to think, and the rewards were remarkable. He now had everything he always wanted, a big house, fast car, and power at his fingertips. However, all this time there had been something else going on, something more sinister. He had become more involved in the dark arts, a form of magic that he'd been dabbling in prior to coming to work for Bella. With her endorsement he had set up a coven of his own; a coven of which he was now the Grand Wizard, a title he revelled in, and the nurse, Mary had been his more recent recruit.

Now in his darkened office, lit by one single black candle and dressed in his Grand Wizards gown adorned with heavy silver jewellery, he proceeded to contact his High Priestess Bella. This was not done in the normal way such as by phone or email but in the only way he knew she would respond, by magic. Within seconds Bella had mounted her broomstick and was speeding through the sky *en route* to the hospital.

By now, Wendy had arrived at the hospital. She was scrambling through the dense undergrowth of the woodland area surrounding the grounds. With her broomstick in hand, she attempted to sweep the brambles to one side. However, her tights had caught on them, and she was feeling slightly peeved.

"Darn these brambles," she muttered, and considered changing back into a crow. She decided against though, as it used up too much of her energy, and far too quickly. She figured she'd need as much as she could muster, and so with ladders in her tights and snags in her cloak she made it to the garden room.

Wendy peered through the window and saw Celeste sat on a chair looking out through the window, not quite in her direction but close. Then, to her dismay she saw a woman walk through the door toward Celeste. The woman was dressed in a smart green tweed dress suit, high heels and her dark hair was tied elegantly in a bun. She recognised her immediately, that face could not be mistaken. She looked very similar to the woman sat in the chair.

"Bella!" She cried and more loudly than she intended.

Hearing Wendy's cry, both women turned and looked in her direction, seeing her face looking at them from behind the glass. Celeste gasped in delight, but Bella screamed like a banshee and charged toward the window, releasing her wand from inside her sleeve and pointing it directly at Wendy. As she did so, Bella's body grew, almost doubling in size, and rising to at least a meter above the floor. As she rose, she spoke an incantation - deep, raspy, and with such emphasis, that each word seemed to have a power of its own. A great flash of light projected out from her wand, splitting the window pain in half, and hitting Wendy in the face. It knocked Wendy off her feet and back onto the hard, concrete floor behind her.

It only took a few seconds for Wendy to come around and when she did, she found both Bella and Celeste were gone. Wendy climbed through the broken window and went in search of them. She passed through the crowded day room, with patients looking on in disbelief at the sight of a stranger wearing a tattered cloak, carrying a broomstick, and with a lump on her forehead the size of an egg. With a finger to her lips, she shushed them to keep quiet and continued through the hospital, up the long cold corridors, sniffing the air in search of the sisters. She followed the scent of Bella and Celeste, which eventually took her to a locked room at the very back of the hospital. The smell of rotting apples was strong now and she felt confident that at least Bella was behind the door. Wendy prepared herself, gripping her wand, she took her flute out of her tatty old bag and opened the door using her own, special magic word.

"TRAZAKENWO!" she shouted, and then the door creaked open.

She was greeted by Emrick and Bella both holding their wand pointed toward her. Celeste was sat in the centre of the room, tied up with what appeared to be enchanted rope and unable to speak or move.

With her wand pointed in their direction, Wendy put her flute to her mouth and played. The tune sounded like wind whistling through the trees, it was beautiful and seemed to resonate around the room causing the windows to rattle and the curtains to blow. Then the wind picked up its pace becoming a whirlwind which gathered momentum until it knocked Emrick and Bella off their feet. They couldn't get up, despite their efforts, instead they crawled on all fours around the room. Wendy pointed her wand at them again. They continued to crawl, but now they were bumping into things, unable to see. They tried to cry out, but no sound came from their mouths.

"RATS!" said Wendy loudly, then one by one thirteen little rats with twitchy noses and sharp claws scrambled from her hat.

They ran toward Emrick and Bella who were now flailing around on the floor trying to get up. First the rats started biting their ankles before working their way up their legs, scratching, gnawing, and nibbling, until they reached their faces and continued attacking them with their claws and teeth. Bella who was now silently screaming, lost concentration and inadvertently released Celeste from her enchanted ropes. The rats then jumped back onto Wendy's hat, and with their little ratty claws they beckoned Celeste to join Wendy who was now waiting by an open window astride her broomstick. Celeste pulled herself up from the floor and jumped quickly onto the back of the broomstick. Within seconds they were flying through the window, with Celeste holding tightly onto Wendy's waist, leaving Emrick and Bella still rolling around and grimacing on the floor.

"Oh Wendy, I've missed you," Celeste whispered to the back of Wendy's hat.

She tightened her grip as they soared high into the night sky. Wendy closed her eyes for a moment and smiled.

"I've missed you too," she said as they flew swiftly over the trees leaving the hospital far behind.

CHAPTER 20

The passengers on the bus were almost at their destination, but that didn't mean they had travelled that far. Rudy had only driven twenty or so miles and was now parked up in a discrete car park on the edge of the National Park. He was concerned that Wendy hadn't shown up yet and thought that it wasn't like her to be late but trusting his instincts he decided to not to concern himself quite yet. He made himself comfy on the front seat and joined the others, who had been asleep on the bus for most of the journey.

Misty was in the middle of the strangest dream. She was lost in a fog and couldn't find her way out. No matter which way she went she would hit a wall, and worse still, she could hear Aunt Bella's deep raspy voice taunting her from the other side.

"Misty I'm here. Misty I'm coming. Misty I'm going to get you!"

The dream was a mixture of intense feelings and vague images, not easy to decipher. At least Misty thought it was a dream.

Am I dreaming or am I awake? She asked, but she had no voice and felt she was silently mouthing the words.

"Misty? Misty, is that you?"

Misty could have sworn she heard someone trying to find her. It didn't sound like Bella as it was a soft, high pitch voice, like that of a young girl and seemed to be coming from behind a wall of fog. She tried to answer back but still had no voice and try as she might, not a sound came out.

"Jump in the air!" She heard the girl say, "Jump as high as you can!"

With all her might Misty tried to jump, but it felt as if she was stuck in treacle.

"I can't," she mouthed, and started to cry.

She felt the wetness of her dream tears fall to her feet around her, and the more she cried the larger the puddle of tears became. Then she started to sink. The puddle had become a lake, and she could feel herself going under. She thought she would drown and began to panic, then she heard Bella's shrill laughter echo in her ears, and she started to sink deeper and deeper. She could still breathe, but it was getting harder. She felt the water fill her lungs and all she could think of at that moment was that she was going to die. Then she heard the girls voice again.

"Breathe in the water," she heard her say. "Become the water."

Misty imagined with all her might that she was dissolving, like a sugar lump in hot tea.

"Keep breathing," the girls voice said. The voice sounded closer now and she no longer heard Bella's raspy cackles, then through the murky water she saw the girl, and she knew her.

Fiona?" She heard her own voice now, but it was gurgling. She saw bubbles rising to the surface, swirling, and popping when they reached the top.

Fiona swam over to Misty, took her hands, and helped her up to surface. Misty gasped and spat out salty brine from her mouth.

"That was a close one," said Fiona, "I thought she had you good 'n proper!"

"Who? Do you mean Bella?" Misty asked, already knowing the answer.

"Who else? She wants you gone, she must know you are the final piece of the puzzle, that's why we need to act quickly." She said with a serious look on her face. "You do know what's going on, don't you?"

Misty looked at her and wanted to say yes but everything was happening so fast that she was finding it difficult to take it all in. She sighed and shook her head.

"Not really," she said.

Fiona smiled kindly at her and led her to the others who had gathered near the stone circle.

"Hey everyone, I found her and she's alright." Fiona called to the others, and they all turned and gave a wave, beckoning them over.

Each of them gave Misty a warm greeting and Mrs Murphy offered her some tea. Misty took a sip and this time she didn't think it tasted too bad since swallowing that salt water.

"What are we waiting for?" Asked Fiona to the others.

Rudy looked flustered and told her that Wendy hadn't arrived yet.

"I don't understand, unless she has business elsewhere," he said. They all nodded and decided she must have a good reason.

Misty still had no idea what was happening and felt a little silly having to ask but decided to anyway.

"Can someone tell me what's going on, please?" They all looked at each other with concerned looks on their faces and huddled into a group to discuss it, but by now Misty had had enough of being kept in the dark and could feel her anger and frustration building up inside her. With her blood now boiling she felt a tingling sensation all through her body, coming out of her fingers. She looked down to see that what were once her feet were now transforming into black claws. They started to poke through her boots which popped off as they grew. Startled by this she looked at her hands and saw that they were beginning to sprout feathers.

"Help! What's going on!" She screamed, then a "CAW, CAW" came from her mouth, which was rapidly transforming into a beak.

Mrs Murphy saw what was happening and shouted to the others.

"Quickly, stop her, she's not ready to transform yet. The time isn't right."

With that they gathered around the half bird half girl and together chanted a spell, repeating it nine times.

"Bird be thou not
Girl thou be
Until time is right
Return to thee."

Misty could feel herself slowing down and returning to her usual form. She wiggled each finger and toe and touched her nose to be sure and did feel quite relieved to be a girl again.

"I think she does need to know what's going on," said Eli, and he stepped toward Misty and knelt at her feet. Then he bowed his head.

"Forgive us," he said, "I for one think you are ready to know the truth."

Misty felt quite humbled by Eli's gesture, and she thanked him by gently tapping his shoulder. He looked up at her, and for a moment she thought she saw someone else looking back at her. His eyes appeared like that of a deer with soft brown fur covering his face, then antlers appeared upon his large thick set forehead. When she blinked, he was Eli again and her heart fluttered. The others were all nodding and agreed to sit her down and explain.

Rudy, however, couldn't settle. He had a feeling that Wendy needed help. After all, it wasn't like her to be late. He excused himself and went back to the bus and sat in the driver's seat. He closed his eyes and focused on Wendy, he imagined all the details of her face, her clothes, her hair, voice, and even her apple crumble smell. He focused on her with such intent that within less than a minute he felt a cool breeze swirling around him. His eyelashes fluttered, and his hair swept off his face.

"Wendy, Wendy, Wendy," he said, then the wind whipped up and swirled around the bus with the sweet smell of apples.

At that same time Wendy was flying through the sky with Celeste on the back of her broomstick, still holding on tightly. She knew time was of the essence, and despite her quickening pace, she would never get to the stones in time. Then she heard a voice calling her name.

Rudy, Rudy, Rudy, she thought, and reached for her flute and played her tune. The wind caught the sound and carried it though the air, whispering and whistling until it reached him. Satisfied they had connected, Rudy cast a spell to bring her even faster.

"Over land and through the air
Blow you fast, Blow you swift
Arrive in time so naught to miss."

Feeling confident that she would arrive in time, Rudy started the bus and headed back to the city, for just after casting the spell he had heard whispering. It sounded like the voice of Shadow in his head, telling him that he was needed elsewhere. Rudy was being told he had to go to Misty's home for something, he couldn't quite make out the details, so decided to trust his instincts and just go. Meanwhile Wendy and Celeste had now accelerated at such a speed and were whizzing through the sky holding on for dear life.

Back at the hospital, the spell had worn off and both Bella and Emrick were brushing themselves down. Bella's witchy ears had also heard the music made by Wendy's flute, and she signalled for Emrick to fetch her broomstick. Bella donned her cloak and hat, and, in a flash, she was off out of the window, into the night sky and following the residual sound of the flute. Emrick watched from the window, then he felt in his pocket for his special key. He had work to do, but first he needed to check on something. This something was getting restless. He could hear groaning noises coming from his cupboard.

"I'm coming Apollyon," he said. "Time for dinner."

CHAPTER 21

There was a shimmering light from the waning moon, which cast shadows on the witches sat within  the stone circle, cross legged and silent. The air was fresh but with the faint smell of cow pats coming from a nearby field. An owl hooted in the distance, and a couple of bats circled above their heads. Misty wasn't sure if she should speak, so said nothing, waiting for someone else to break the ice. She was surprised when Sami was the first to speak, as he appeared quite shy and a man of few words.

"All of us here are walkers between the worlds," he said. "We were all born with that gift. Some of us have been walking for many years, and over many lifetimes. Some of us have learned it more recently. Each of us has been selected for a specific purpose, and we all have an important part to play, especially now as there are dark forces at work."

Everyone nodded in agreement. Sami continued.

"I am fairly new to this, but I know what my role is. I am the deliverer of messages, through words and symbols. I have also been waiting for you to be ready, Misty. Each day on my round I have kept watch and let Wendy know how you're doing." Then he turned to Mavis Allgood, giving her a nod to continue.

Mavis looked at Misty and smiled.

"Well, you know me, don't you?" She giggled and continued.

"When you came to Willowbrook High, I was sent by Wendy to ensure your wellbeing, to make sure that you stay fit and healthy. I have been a healer for hundreds of years, over many incarnations, each time returning to continue my purpose. Each time, I feel I am getting wiser and stronger." Mavis nodded to Albert Woolley, who turned to Misty to speak.

"My role was always to guide you with knowledge, to ensure you didn't stray from the path that was chosen for you. Your father didn't know this, but Wendy guided him to send you to Willowbrook because I was there. You see, we have been friends for many years," he said and winked at Misty, who was beginning to find the whole thing too incredible for words. He then turned to Eli.

"I have been protecting you, a bit like a bodyguard," Eli said shrugging his muscly shoulders. "You never saw me, but I intervened on a few occasions when you were almost attacked."

Misty couldn't believe it.

"Attacked by who?" She asked.

"Bella of course, she has been hunting you down for the past five years, but she only just found out where you were living. She was trying to get to you before you changed, hoping she could stop you before you knew the truth." Eli explained.

Misty felt sick, the thought of all this going on without her knowledge was overwhelming.

"Changed?" She asked.

"Yes, before you became a witch," replied Eli.

"Did my father know what was going on?" She asked.

"Your father has been keeping you away from Bella since your mum and brother were taken by her, moving you from place to place. But he knew that the day would come when she would find you, and he was frightened she would take you too. I'm not sure what else he knows, but I'm certain he has done his best to protect you," he said.

Misty sat there staring at Eli. She had always been a little scared of him, with his large stature, big muscles, and tattoos. He looked like he could kill someone just by looking at them but seeing him now, she saw a big man with kind eyes who seemed to exude a serenity that she hadn't noticed before. He made her feel very safe. She thought then of her father, she had no idea he had been trying his best to protect her too.

Jabir was next, and he stood up. He had a big smile on his face and spoke in a way that made it was obvious he was trying to lighten the mood.

"I am not just a barber. I am a magician of the hair!" He said. "I use hair for spell craft which has helped keep your father safe, and you, of course."

She remembered then how he would cut her father's hair and recalled the time she saw him put some of the hair in his pocket. She had thought it was strange at the time.

"Thank you, Jabir," she said, and still smiling, he sat down again.

Next Kitty Bloom, the plump-faced dinner lady spoke.

"Those extra helpings? Well, they were laced with good magic, keeping you healthy." She said.

"Wendy and me, cook together all the time. She makes a mean apple crumble!" She laughed loudly and the others joined in.

Misty was smiling now as she thought of all those puddings. Everyone then turned to look at Ariana the librarian. Misty had never seen her smile, let alone laugh before, and there she was chuckling and snorting like a totally different person.

"Shush!" she said to Misty and laughed even more. "Well, I'm the keeper of the books, I guard the sacred texts and make sure they don't fall into the wrong hands," she said.

"It's nearly happened a few times, that Charlie was becoming a bit of a nuisance." She looked into Misty's eyes. "I'm sorry he betrayed you. I know you liked him a lot," she said and held out her hand to her. Misty took it, held it for a moment, and felt a sadness creep over her.

"Thanks, that means a lot," she said and wiped a tear away.

"Who's next?" asked Mrs Murphy. No one replied.

"Me then?" she said jokingly. "I'm not just a sweet shop lady. My real craft is potions and lotions. What you see out the front of my shop is just for show, and for the kiddies. I like to keep an eye out for them, you know. You especially Misty, those sweets you been eating, well they been opening your eyes as well as giving you fillings," she said with a titter, and kept chuckling to herself until interrupted by Myla who jumped up and gave a twirl.

"I Misty am the dance," and she proceeded to whirl around and around until she became a blur. Misty looked on so mesmerised by her movement that she was no longer saddened by the thought of Charlie. Then Myla stopped whirling and smiled her big scarlet lipped smile. Everyone clapped and cheered.

"It brings happiness and pleasure, but it can also take you places. I can teach you my craft one day, if you would like?" she said and blew her a kiss.

"I would love to know how to dance." Misty said smiling.

Then everyone went silent and looked at Fiona. She was sat as quiet as a mouse with her head tilted back and her eyes closed. Then her body quivered, and bright colourful light shimmered around her, sparkling through her tiny frame. Something remarkable happened next, Fiona's body seemed to melt into a pool of translucent liquid, and beneath it rose a being so beautiful it took Misty's breath away.

Misty gasped as she saw little fragile Fiona's transformation and watched as the shimmering being flitted from stone to stone before settling back down amongst the group and transforming back to her human form.

"Wow!" was the only word that Misty said as she waited for Fiona to speak.

"I am Fey, or fairy if you like," Fiona explained. "I spend most of my time between the worlds. Believe it or not I am older than Wendy. I knew one of your ancestors. I believe she was your great, great, great, great grandmother, and she helped to save my life. My kind were almost wiped out, centuries ago by those in power who were afraid of us. I was one of the few who survived. I owe your ancestor my life now, and I am here to protect you." Fiona said and bowed her head to her.

Then there was silence and, everyone's eyes turned to Misty. She felt an obligation to say something, but she had no story to tell. At least nothing they didn't already know about.

"I don't know what to say, the last few weeks have been too weird, and now I've met all of you and you've all been helping me, I suppose what I mean is, well ... Thank you." She looked around and everyone was smiling at her, but she realised there was a face missing from the crowd.

"Where's Rudy?" she asked, noticing the bus driver's absence.

"Oh, the Old Gods!" said Mrs Murphy with a worried look.

"Indeed, where *is* he?" Said Jabir.

"And Wendy should be here by now." Said Ariana.

"Chernabog's hammer! The bus is gone!" shouted Eli who had run down to check.

The witches sensed trouble. They knew that Rudy wouldn't have left them unless he had good reason, or unless he was taken, but they knew exactly what to do. They started building a fire in the centre of the circle, then together placed a large metal cauldron on the edge of the circle, laying out all sorts of ingredients next to it.

Misty could see different types of dried plants, bottles filled with different coloured liquids, a tub of salt and various other items that she couldn't identify. She looked on as they each busied themselves with different tasks and wondered what her role would be. She felt too shy to ask, so instead she went to help Mrs Murphy organise the dried plants.

"Interested in herbs, are we?" Mrs Murphy asked with a sharp look in her eye.

"Um, probably. I don't know much about them." Misty replied feebly.

"Ha! We'll make a proper witch out of you yet." Mrs Murphy said and began explaining the names and uses for the ones she had prepared.

Misty tried to look interested but was distracted by other, more worrying matters.

"How are herbs going to fight my Aunt Bella?" she said and started to cry. The tears streamed down her face, and she tried to wipe them away with her hand but ended up with snot running down her arm.

"There, there dear," said Mrs Murphy, and gave her a tissue from her pocket. It smelled funny, like rotten eggs, but Misty used it, nonetheless.

"Sit down over there and close your eyes, it'll all be alright." Mrs Murphy pointed at a space by the largest stone. Misty did as she was told and made herself comfortable, and before long her eyes became heavy, and she drifted off into a deep sleep.

CHAPTER 22

Wendy was making good time as she rapidly headed north to the stone circle. With the aid of Rudy's spell and the strong south wind it meant that even with the extra weight of Celeste on the back she was able to navigate the sky with ease.

"Where are we going?" asked Celeste, who was still very weak but starting to feel a little more like herself now that she was away from her captors. "Are you taking me home?"

Wendy thought for a moment, looked up at the stars to check their position. She licked her finger and held it up above her head to check if the wind direction was still southerly, and then decided to take a detour.

"Yes, but I think there's somewhere we need to go first." She brought her broomstick to a stop and turned east, heading towards the city.

A few miles behind them, heading north was Bella. Although she wasn't as experienced a witch as Wendy. She was, however, an excellent broomstick rider with an even better sense of smell, but most importantly her anger made her broomstick go faster and right now, she was raging. Suddenly she smelt something, and she too changed direction, following the sweet scent of apples.

Rudy was still driving, and every now and then he would stop and check the sky. Fortunately, it was a clear night, and the stars were bright. He had a good sense of direction, but also used the elements to guide him. Tonight, the wind was whispering the way and leading him where he needed to go. Before long, he was back in the city and heading toward the housing estate. The tower blocks were drawing nearer, but he only had a vague idea as to where Misty lived, so he parked up and waited for a sign. It was dark outside, and if it wasn't for the streetlights he wouldn't have noticed the black cat curled up on the bin bag. He got out and approached him.

"Shadow?" He said, and the cat yawned and stretched.

"Hi Rudy," he said. "Follow me."

So, Rudy followed.

Robert had been extremely pleased to see Michael, as the past five years of separation, from both his wife and son had taken its toll, and he was not the man he once was. Seeing Michael again, albeit in a terrible state, had lifted his spirits. Both father and son were sat together on the sofa drinking hot cocoa and munching toasted tea cakes when there was a knock at the door.

"Misty?" Robert said hopefully, jumping up and tripping over his slippers as he rushed to answer it. He opened the door and saw a stranger dressed in a witch's costume stood next to a black fluffy cat. His heart sank.

"Can we come in?" asked Rudy, and without waiting for an answer they entered.

"Who are you?" asked Michael, staring up at this blond, curly haired, rather handsome looking man dressed in a brown cloak and pointed hat. There was also a black fluffy cat with sparkly green eyes sat licking his paws by his side. Robert was nervously scratching his head, not knowing what on earth was happening. First his daughter goes missing, then his son appears and now this.

"No time to explain." Rudy began, "I'm here because of Misty."

"Where is she? Is she alright?" asked Robert frantically.

"You'd just better come with me, and I'll take you to her," said Rudy.

Shadow stopped washing himself and padded over to the bed. He sniffed around and immediately found Celeste's cloak, hat, and wand that were hidden from sight.

"Bring these with you," said Shadow to Michael. Without giving the talking cat a second thought, Michael found a bag and put them inside. Then Robert and Michael left the flat, following Rudy and Shadow outside.

Robert knew better than to question a man wearing a cloak and pointed hat. He'd married a witch after all and guessed that this must have something to do with Bella, so decided to trust him, especially if it meant taking him to Misty. He'd already tried and failed to get anything sensible out of Michael, but he had learned that something terrible had gone on at Charlie's flat. As they got nearer to where Charlie lived, Robert stopped and considered knocking the door, to *have a word,* but Michael stopped him.

"You can sort him out another time, Dad," he said, pulling his sleeve.

Robert nodded and agreed. That would be for another day. They continued walking, following the brown cloaked witch with the talking black cat.

Overhead, thick clouds formed, and cold rain started to fall. Rudy stopped walking for a moment and looked up. In the corner of his eye. He spotted two broomsticks being flown behind the clouds. He strained his eyes for a better look, but they had already gone.

"Is anything going on up there?" asked Robert, also looking up at the sky.

Rudy looked at Shadow and raised his eyebrows knowingly.

"Did you see what I saw?" he asked.

"She's there." Shadow replied coolly. "We should wait on the bus," he instructed, and continued trotting along the pavement.

"Excellent!" Rudy exclaimed, and with an encouraging smile he ushered Robert and Michael to follow. They looked at each other, and feeling a strange mixture of confusion, worry and excitement, they said nothing and silently followed Rudy and Shadow to the bus.

High above the tower blocks, there was more than a storm brewing. There was a commotion in the skies. Bella had caught up with Wendy and Celeste, and they were now fighting like only witches do, with magic.

Bella uttered the most hideous incantation, and the cold rain froze. Hailstones the size of golf balls began to fall from the clouds. Bella screeched and cackled with delight whenever Celeste cried out in pain as they struck her. Wendy tried her best to dodge them, but they kept coming harder and faster, each one stinging worse than a wasp.

Using her wand to bat the hailstones away, Wendy took her broomstick high above the clouds and waited for the right moment. When she saw Bella approach from below, she aimed her broomstick and dive-bombed her with such a terrifying force that Bella almost toppled off her broomstick. Hanging on with one hand, Bella pulled herself back onto her broomstick and continued her chase.

Ducking and diving, Wendy managed to dodge the hailstones and out manoeuvre Bella. With Celeste clinging on for her life, Wendy raised her wand above her head and uttered a special, most secret incantation. Then with a swipe of her wand she aimed a flash of lightening right at Bella's broomstick, causing it to crack in two. Bella came tumbling down and landed in a heap on a tower block roof, with her broken broomstick following her.

Dazed but undeterred, Bella looked at her broken broomstick and screamed. Then she grabbed the two pieces and uttered a spell to mend it. When it was fixed, she headed by foot to Misty's flat, determined she would not be defeated.

When Bella arrived at the flat, she uttered her magic word to open the door, but when she entered, she realised she was too late. The flat was empty. There were just two half-drunk cocoas on the table, still warm.

They can't be far, she thought.

By now, Wendy and Celeste were outside Charlie's flat. Celeste, weary with it all, was holding Wendy's arm, and trying her hardest not to collapse in a heap. Wendy knocked the door.

"TRAZAKENWO!" She shouted, and blew, a slow but powerful blow. The breeze that came from Wendy's mouth got bigger and bigger, like a storm forming from her lips. It became a huge blast of wind which tore down the door.

Behind the shattered door stood Charlie's mother, her eyes ablaze and her mouth quivering. Charlie and the rest of the coven were stood behind her, all armed with their wands. However, the howling wind continued to flow from Wendy's mouth. It engulfed them and knocked them off their feet.

148

Paralysed, they all lay on the floor unable to move.

"That'll do." Wendy said with a chuckle. Satisfied that Bella's coven were incapacitated, at least for now, she took Celeste back out through the doorway and onto the street.

Bella saw them. She was stood, holding her broomstick, on a nearby rooftop ready to pounce. She swiftly mounted her broomstick and swooped down, with such force that she was able to grab Celeste from Wendy's arm and carry her away. Hanging on with her spindly arms, Celeste had no choice but to cling to her sister, terrified and with tears streaming down her face, she watched Wendy disappear from sight.

Dismayed that her plan was thwarted, Wendy mounted her broomstick to take chase. As she was about to leave, Shadow appeared from around the corner and bounded toward her.

"There is no time! You will have to let her go, for now," he said. Wendy shook her head. "I had her and lost her again." She said sadly. But knowing that time was ticking by far too quickly, she relented and followed Shadow to the waiting bus.

Rudy spotted Wendy and Shadow as they came around the corner. Relieved and excited to see them, he alerted them with a toot of his horn.

"Wendy. Thank the Gods, GET ON!" he shouted. "And meet Michael and Robert."

CHAPTER 23

Wendy tried her best to appear cheerful at Rudy's introductions, but time was running out. She had planned the ceremony to take place at exactly midnight and it was getting on for eleven fifteen. That was nowhere near enough time, and with Celeste gone it wasn't going to be quite as she'd foreseen it in her vision. For the first time in centuries, Wendy was experiencing doubt.

Distracted with thoughts that she may have screwed things up, Wendy put her feet up on the back of the seat in front, closed her eyes and with the motion of the bus it wasn't long before she was sound asleep. Rudy had started the bus and headed back the way he had come. Michael and Robert were sat on the front seats, wondering where they were going. Shadow was curled up and purring by their feet, all in all, it seemed a peculiar situation.

Robert had recognised Wendy as soon as she boarded the bus as he had met her several times over the years. He also knew how much Celeste loved her and that was a good enough reason for him to trust her, even if she did unnerve him a little. Michael also recognised her, having met her when Misty was born. She had come to their house with a present for her and he remembered feeling jealous of the attention she gave the squawking baby in the crib. This memory was so vivid, but he couldn't understand why he couldn't recall anything else from his life before Aunt Bella took him. He knew that it was his father sat next to him, he knew his sister was Misty, but he couldn't recall his mother's face, and right now that saddened him.

Michael thought about Aunt Bella, the chores she made him do, the punishments when he disobeyed her, oh and the rituals. Yes, the rituals and magic, although she had taught him no magic in that time. He guessed that she had thought he would use it against her. Aunt Bella had drummed it into him that he was only there to serve her as a slave and a prisoner. He was often kept in a cold bare room with no food for days and he remembered the bitter potions she made him drink, and the stomach cramps that came afterwards. He remembered running away. He didn't get far and gave up trying in the end as he knew he would never escape her clutches. Michael sat and recalled it all, his mind flooded with painful memories. The fear was the worst, he thought he would die on so many occasions that he just gave in and learned to forget his life before her. Yes, that was it. He forgot everything so he could survive, afraid he would die of a broken heart.

Michael wanted to cry. He wanted to sob, snotty sobby tears, but he couldn't. He seemed to have forgotten how to do that too. He looked down at the bag that he had packed earlier and took out the cards and shuffled them. He also remembered the cards had been his only solace in his isolation, and that he had played solitaire for hours on end. He had come to think of the cards as his friends and would have conversations with them. They would almost come alive in his hands as he talked to them about his problems. The Jack of Spades was his favourite, and his least favourite was the Queen of Hearts. She could make him sad. The Joker could be a nightmare sometimes, but at least he could be fun. Michael chuckled to himself as he recalled the time when the Joker had played a trick on the Seven of Clubs, when he had tried to run away. Michael had to intervene before the Joker was ripped in half. Now he sat on the bus shuffling and thinking. He decided to pick a card at random, something he often did when he didn't know what else to do. He would try to see what the card wanted to tell him. It gave him some comfort at least. Closing his eyes, he selected a card and turned it over. In his hand was the Queen of Hearts. His heart sank. *Damn it,* he thought, *my worst card.*

He studied the Queen for a moment and there before his eyes he started to see his mother's face slowly appear. That was her, surely? Yes, there she was smiling back at him, her face as clear as day.

"Mum?" He said out loud to the card.

Shadow's ears pricked when he heard Michael and he jumped up on the seat between him and his now sleeping father.

"You know the magic of the cards Michael? If so, then you know what to do." Said Shadow.

Not really sure if he had imagined the cat talking to him, Michael continued, staring intently at the card, totally mesmerised. Then he started talking to her, telling her how much he missed her and how much he wanted her with him. Shadow satisfied that he had conveyed his message jumped down and went over to Wendy who was still snoring loudly.

"Wake up, wake up, wake up," he said, and tapped her with his front paw. "Celeste, she's here."

Wendy woke abruptly.

"Celeste? Where is she?" She asked looking over to Michael who was now deep in conversation with his mother.

"Give me the card, quickly," she instructed him, and he did as she asked, albeit a little reluctantly. Wendy took the card in her left hand and took out her flute in the other. She played her usual tune, and the air around them turned cool. A breeze fluttered through the bus, the windows rattled, and the breeze became a gust and then a huge wind, which tore a hole in the roof. With that, Wendy was gone, through the hole and away. Rudy looked at the hole above his head and saw the silhouette of a crow flying into the night sky. A black feather landed on his face, making him sneeze, and he smiled.

"Go Wendy, fly like the wind," he said quietly to himself and continued the route back to the stones.

The commotion disturbed Robert from his sleep.

"What's going on?" He asked Michael.

It seemed to him that he was in the dark with everything right now, and although intrigued, he guessed that it was witchcraft stuff. He had been used to it before Celeste and Michael were taken, when everything used to make sense. Before he turned to the bottle.

Michael looked at his father and with his lips trembling and his eyes now wet with tears, told him how he had seen his mother.

"She appeared to me on a playing card, it was the Queen of Hearts. I saw her face and she told me she was with Aunt Bella and that she was in danger," he said with tears now streaming down his red cheeks and landing in his lap.

"The Queen of Hearts you say? Yes, that was your mum's card, you've done well Michael. Don't ask me to explain any of this as I haven't got a clue, but if she's contacted you then I'm sure it's a good sign," and he patted his son on the knee.

"Dad, I think I need to do something more. I'm sure of it. If Mum is the Queen of Hearts, do you think Aunt Bella is a card? What if she's the, I don't know, the Joker? Or the Queen of Spades? Perhaps I could contact her too?" Michael suddenly felt hopeful for the first time in years, and he knew he could do something to help. "But which one is she?" He mumbled whilst shuffling the pack.

At the same time Wendy was closing in. She had picked up the scent of rotten apples and was flying east. She spotted Bella, still on her broomstick with Celeste on the back. The other witches were not far behind her, with Charlie sitting on the back of his mother's broomstick. They were almost back at the hospital, and Wendy could kick herself for not ensuring a more enduring incapacitation spell.

Wendy followed the witches to the hospital and to the open window of Emrick's office. She flew down onto a nearby tree with a clear view and watched. Being a crow had its advantages, meaning she could easily go undetected, but shape shifting used up her vital energy resources, so she knew she had to be extra wise. Wendy spotted Bella and Celeste through the window. She could see Emrick and others with them. She hopped closer to get a better view.

"Oh widdershins! What are they doing in there?" She squawked when she realised that Charlie and his mother, and the rest of Bella's coven were there too, all sitting in a circle, with Emrick performing some hideous incantation. Wendy knew she had to act quickly.

While trying to come up with a plan, Wendy thought it best that she shapeshifted back into her human form. Unfortunately, she hadn't brought her broomstick with her and had no idea how she could get Celeste out of there-and to the stones in time. Trusting her instincts, she turned herself back and shook the feathers from off her boots. She jumped down from the tree and headed to the main entrance of the hospital. Wendy boldly walked along the corridors and before long she was outside Emrick's office door, her wand in her right hand ready to strike.

Back on the bus, Michael had made progress. He truly believed he could do this again and concentrated on seeing Aunt Bella's face. Going through the deck, he waited for it to appear on a card. It didn't take long. When he held the Queen of Spades in his hand, his fingers trembled and the card started to shake, and there it was. Her face staring back at him, grimacing, and squirming like she was trying to escape, but held hostage in his hand.

"Ha! Now I've got YOU!" Michael screamed at her. His fear of her evaporated and a new sense of confidence filled his being. He stood up from his seat and held the card above his head.

"You WILL be defeated." Michael told the card, and ripped it in two, tearing his Aunt Bella's head from her body.

Wendy was still outside Emrick's door when she heard violent screams come from inside. With her wand still ready to strike, she uttered her magic word.

"TRAZAKENWO!" A huge gust of wind blew the door off its hinges and onto the floor with a thud, knocking over at least three of the witches. Wendy stood at the doorway, eyes blazing red, ready for a fight, ready for anything, but she needn't have been. Michael had not only found Aunt Bella, but he had also found Emrick and the others in his deck. They all lay on the floor, immobile, unable to move or even speak. Bella was motionless, like a statue, still holding her neck with her hands. Stood next to her, holding Emrick's broomstick, was Celeste.

"You took your time Wend," she said with a smile. "Come on, let's go."

Celeste stood astride the broomstick and beckoned Wendy to join her. Seconds later the pair were flying off into the night, this time Celeste taking the helm with Wendy behind, holding on tightly.

CHAPTER 24

Celeste hadn't ridden a broomstick for years, so it felt wonderful to be soaring through the sky again. She whooped and shrieked and called out to the Gods that she was back. She almost forgot that Wendy was holding on behind until she prodded Celeste with her wand and told her to slow down, just a little. Celeste felt like her old self again, the magic had returned in abundance, and she felt surges of energy fill her being until she felt full to the brim and super charged. Wendy felt a mixture of jubilation and relief, she should never have doubted her vision as it was now all coming together. Now all they had to do was reach the stone circle in less than ten minutes.

The bus was almost there too. It would likely take the same time to arrive as Wendy and Celeste if Rudy put his foot down. Shadow could sense that they were getting close and started to purr as loud as a motorbike. Michael stroked his head and told him how grateful he was, that he couldn't have done it without his help. Shadow nodded and blinked, his green eyes sparkling. Robert retrieved the bag which held Celeste's cloak, hat, and wand from under the seat, and asked Shadow what he should do with them.

"She will need them," he said, and carried on purring. Robert stared back in disbelief.

Wendy spotted the bus approaching the stones and instructed Celeste to land.

"What? Actually, *on* the bus?" Celeste asked, thinking she was teasing her.

"Definitely *on* the bus. See that hole on the roof? Aim for that," said Wendy.

Celeste skilfully manoeuvered the broomstick at the exact angle required for them to enter the bus directly through the hole.

The shock of seeing Wendy and Celeste enter the bus, still on the broomstick and through the ceiling almost caused Rudy to crash into a ditch. As for Robert and Michael, it was the most amazing, incredibly wonderful thing for them to witness. The reunion consisted of intense hugs, kisses, and tears of joy. Celeste held Michael in her arms and looked at his tear-stained face.

"Thank you, my boy, I am so proud of you," she said as she wiped his cheeks with her hand.

"Is it really you?" Robert gazed into Celeste eyes and saw the beautiful woman he had always loved. "You really are the most beautiful witch I have ever seen." He said as he looked her up and down, admiring every inch of her.

Celeste kissed him on the lips, and it felt like they had never been apart. The love they felt for each other was still as strong as ever and they kissed again. Michael felt embarrassed seeing his parents kissing and made a point of reminding them he was there. They stopped, looked around and remembered where they were. Everyone laughed together. Then Celeste noticed the bag on the seat.

"What's this?" She said knowingly as she pulled out her belongings. "Now I really am ready." She put on her jade green cloak and hat and held her wand firmly in her right hand.

"Right then Rudy, what's the time?" asked Wendy as the bus came to a stop.

"Thirty minutes to midnight," he replied.

"Just in time." Wendy grinned and led the way off the bus and towards the stones.

Misty was still sleeping. Earlier on Mrs Murphy had gently kissed her forehead and whispered *"sweet dreams"* in her ear, leaving her by the largest stone, covered with a warm woollen blanket.

As soon as Misty had fallen asleep, she had the strangest experience. It felt like she had woken up again. She felt her body rise into the air and she could see everything going on around her. When she looked down, she realised she was floating above her sleeping self, the woollen blanket still wrapped tightly around her.

161

Misty panicked for a moment and wondered if she had died, but she could hear her heartbeat loudly as if it was booming in her ears, and a tight sensation around her belly button, so she guessed she was still alive. Then she heard a faint sound coming from beyond the stone circle and noticed an owl swoop down, almost silently, and come to perch on the tallest stone. The owl was white with brown markings, and it had a heart shaped face. She thought it was so beautiful. It hooted three times and flew in the direction of a field not far away, coming to rest on a wooden post.

Misty found herself intrigued and floated over to it. She wondered if it was trying to tell her something, so she asked it if it had a name. The owl said nothing, just looked at her with eyes black as coal, then blinked and flew off into the field. Misty followed, still floating, but now the air felt thick, like soup. She used her arms as if she was swimming.

Misty followed the ghost-like bird until she came to the edge of a forest. Before her was a gate. It was made of wood and had some markings on it. She immediately recognised them as Runes but had no idea what they meant.

The owl elegantly landed on the gate and before her eyes it transformed into a woman. The woman seemed very old. She had many lines on her face and was bent over, as though her back was crooked. Her fingers were nobbled, and she had silver rings on each one. She was dressed in a black gown with the hood up, and Misty could see long white hair underneath it.

Misty stared at the woman, and the woman smiled. She had eyes that sparkled, shining green, like pools of water. When she opened her mouth, her teeth were as white as pearls. Misty thought this old woman was going to open the gate for her, so she moved closer as if to go through, but the woman shook her head. Then she held out her hand and when Misty took it in her own, her hearing became sharper than it had ever been.

Misty could hear all the sounds of the forest behind the gate, in unison: mice scurrying, the badgers and the foxes foraging. She could hear the trees swaying and talking to each other, fungi popping up through the ground, and she could hear every word the witches were saying back at the stone circle. Misty marvelled at this gift and wondered if it would last forever. Then the woman spoke.

Her voice sounded like running water, but Misty understood every word.

"I am the Goddess of the Crossroads. I am the weaver of the spaces between worlds, and I will be your guide. When you are ready, I will open the gate."

With that, she transformed back into the owl and flew into the forest.

Misty felt herself sucked back into her sleeping body, and she sat bolt upright. Her heart was beating fast, and her skin was wet with sweat. She looked around and saw the witches sat around a fire in the centre of the stone circle. She could hear them singing, so she sat there watching them for a few minutes, trying to calm herself from her peculiar dream.

Myla got up and began dancing around the fire, twirling, and spinning around and around. The light of the fire and the smoke blowing around made the scene look calm and serene. Misty wanted to join them, so she got up and went to sit between Mavis Allgood and Fiona. They all welcomed her into the circle with a nod and a smile. Soon, Misty was singing with them, a song that she did not know, yet she somehow knew the words.

Misty looked around and noticed that Rudy was still missing.

And where was Wendy? she wondered. Before she could ask their whereabouts, out of the corner of her eye she saw the shapes of five people and a cat. They were walking toward the circle, and as they came closer, they emerged out of the darkness to reveal who they were. Misty's heart was beating so fast now she thought it would burst. As the group approached the light of the fire, she could see their faces. Faces of the people she loved the most.

Misty jumped up and leapt over Fiona's head and ran to them. Her family, whom she thought she would never see again, were now all together once more. It was so unimaginable that she thought she might still be dreaming so she pinched herself.

Ouch, yes, she was definitely awake.

Celeste, Robert, and Michael hugged Misty tightly. Misty noticed her father's face was wet with tears, but he looked happy. She noticed that her mother was dressed in her cloak and hat. Her face glowed and her eyes sparkled, just as she was before she was taken away. Then there was Michael, his eyes were bright, and his face shone with happiness. Watching the family reunion, Wendy and Rudy grinned at each other, and together they all joined the circle.

"Now we can begin," announced Wendy, and beckoned Eli to join her. They both left the circle and stood either side of the fire. Shadow wandered off and made a bed from Mrs Murphy's blanket, whilst Misty, eyes wide open, looked on in wonder. She heard her name being called which made her jump. Looking round, she realised it was Wendy who had said her name. Misty noticed that she looked different, she blinked, looking at her again.

Wendy's voice sounded strange, deep, and raspy. Misty shuddered as she saw Wendy raise her arms up like wings and again said her name.

"Misty." Wendy paused, and then asked, "What is the time?"

"It's ten minutes to midnight." Misty said, without hesitation.

"Perfect," said Wendy.

CHAPTER 25

There was intense activity for the next ten minutes. Time was playing its usual trick, and it seemed like ten hours. Apart from Misty, Michael, and Robert, the others were wearing individually coloured cloaks and pointed hats. It was chilly despite the clouded sky, and the only light came from the fire. Myla was still dancing, spiralling around and around the fire like a coiled spring, becoming more frenzied with each spin, and everyone watched, captivated by her, totally entranced by her perfect display of movement. On closer observation, Misty noticed the air within the circle was also spinning, with iridescent colours swirling and shimmering like oil spilled in a puddle. Misty and Michael looked on in awe and both held out their hands to touch this colourful swirling energy only to find it evaporated in their grasp and then continued to move swiftly around the circle.

Mavis had a large bowl of water which she sprinkled around the outside of the stone circle. Misty could hear her chanting as she did it but couldn't quite make out the words. Mavis then approached each person and flicked water on them, saying "be thou cleansed." Misty thought it peculiar that a sprinkle of water could cleanse you, but she thanked her anyway.

Albert and Kitty brought out a large heavy cauldron. It was black with little metal feet on the bottom, and they placed it in the centre of the circle, between Wendy and Eli, who were stood together, eyes closed and holding hands. Using metal tongs, they retrieved some black burned wood from the fire and placed this red-hot charcoal inside the cauldron before returning to join the circle. Mrs Murphy had brought bunches of dried herbs which she placed into the smoking cauldron. As they dropped onto the hot embers, they turned into aromatic incense which swirled up into the air and engulfed them all. Misty closed her eyes and inhaled deeply. The smell was intoxicating, and it made her feel a little giddy. She opened one eye and noticed Jabir lift a drum that he had previously been resting his elbow on. Misty watched as he closed his eyes, puffed out his chest then with all his might he beat it with two leather bound sticks. It produced a sound like a beating heart. The rhythmic boom, boom, boom, echoed so fiercely creating a powerful atmosphere that seemed to increase the speed of the swirling air and smoke surrounding them.

Michael nudged Misty and nodded for her to look at their parents who were sat together, smiling lovingly at each other. It made Michael and Misty feel very content to know they were all together again, despite the strangeness of it all. Then their mum started to hum a tune. She started quietly becoming louder and louder as others joined in, it sounded familiar, but they couldn't quite put their fingers on it. Maybe it was the lullaby that sent them to sleep when they were little. They joined in and in time with the beat of the drum they hummed the familiar tune, sounding like a musical swarm of bees. Misty turned to whisper something to Michael but saw that he had fallen asleep, his head was resting on his knees, so she turned him onto his side and made him comfortable. Celeste smiled at her and mouthed "*thank you.*" Misty then realised that her mum had already settled her father down beside her and he too was sleeping soundly.

Ariana was sat quietly with a book on her lap. She opened it and flicked through the pages until she found the one she was after, taking it over to Sami before returning to her space in the circle. The humming and the drumming stopped, and Sami stood up and addressed them all by name, and then he thanked the four cardinal points of North, South, East, and West. He thanked the four elements of earth, air, fire, and water, and then he thanked the fifth element of spirit. He thanked the Horned God and Moon Goddess, before finally introducing Wendy as *"Mother."* She stepped forward.

Sami sat back down still holding the book. Wendy took salt from a drawstring bag she was holding and circled the group sprinkling it around them until it made a full circle. Then Wendy stood with her eyes to the sky, watching the moon slide out from behind the clouds. The light fell on her face, giving it a warm yellow glow. Wendy stretched her spine and Misty marvelled as she saw her change. She seemed to grow taller and become slimmer. Wendy shook her head and long dark tresses of shiny hair fell from beneath her pointed hat and settled around her shoulders. Her lips seemed fuller, and her few wrinkles disappeared. Misty gasped and stared as Wendy continued to transform into this younger version of herself.

As Wendy stood there getting younger from the light from the moon, Eli stepped forward and produced a large metal sword from a sheath that he had hung around his waist. He held it up above his head and spoke.

"I am Lord of the Hunt!" His voice was deep and so loud the ground vibrated. A thunderous roar came from within the forest and surrounding hills. It shook the ground like an earthquake and Misty thought for a moment that it would open up and swallow her. But despite her fear she sat as still as she could until the shaking stopped. Eli continued.

"We are gathered here to witness the dawn of a new era," his voice echoed around the circle, then he placed his sword back in its sheath before taking it off and placing it gently on the floor.

Misty stared at him in amazement. Her jaw dropped and she thought she would cry out but managed to stifle her yelp. He didn't look at all like the large, tattooed biker with long straggly hair, he too was transforming. Before her now stood a giant of a man, wearing just leaf green breeches, his cape and hat falling to the floor. Soft brown fur covered his top half and the muscles in his arms rippled as he flexed them. His eyes were black and shiny, and his ears pointed. Misty watched as horns emerged from his broad skull and formed into magnificent antlers, and his feet became hooves. Eli looked remarkable as he stood there, half man, half stag, with a presence that took her breath away. Misty looked around at each individual and realised she didn't really know them, not really. She had only just started seeing that they were special, but a man becoming a stag, that, was something else.

"Misty." She heard her name being called but was still in shock so didn't respond.

"Misty?" Then she recognised the voice and realised Wendy was addressing her.

"Come here child." Wendy beckoned her to join them by the fire. "Tell us the time."

Misty knew the answer but suddenly felt scared. Her heart started pounding and she felt the colour drain from her cheeks. She didn't want to get up, she just wanted to sit quietly and watch. Her mother tapped her knee.

"Go on, it's alright," she said reassuringly.

Misty got up, and as she approached the transformed Wendy and the Lord of the Hunt she felt her knees buckle beneath her and she fell to the floor in front of them.

"It's midnight," she mumbled before passing out.

Celeste went forward and made sure she was comfortable. She placed a blanket over Misty and kissed her cheek before returning to her place in the circle whilst the others continued with the ceremony.

As soon as Misty had said those words, she felt something shift inside her. Something was drawn out of her body, and she saw herself fall to the floor as if she was looking from above.

Ah, oh here we go again, Misty thought as she found herself floating above the stone circle, looking down at her mum placing the blanket over her and kissing her cheek. She could see the rest of the witches sat quietly with their hands out and palms facing up, all, except Wendy and The Lord of the Hunt who were stood with their arms crossed over their chests. Misty hovered above them, and Wendy looked up and their eyes met. Wendy grinned and winked at her, eyes sparkling. Then Misty heard her say something to her, but it was too muffled to understand so using her arms she swam through the swirling air to get closer.

"Think of your feet." Wendy said. Misty definitely heard her this time.

"Why?" Was all Misty could think to say.

"When you want to return to your body, think of your feet. Now go." said Wendy, her voice gurgled, like she was underwater.

"Ok, think of my feet," said Misty to herself. Then she heard the hoot of an owl and in the corner of her eye she saw a flash of white. The barn owl was back, and so she followed it.

CHAPTER 26

Back at the hospital, Mary entered Emrick's office to find the witches writhing around on the floor, in agony and unable to speak. Bella was so contorted that her head now faced the wrong way, and she was desperately trying to turn it back, whilst Emrick was slithering like a snake on his belly. Charlie reminded her of an upturned tortoise. He was laying on his back unable to move his limbs, rocking himself back and forth, in an attempt to get up, his teeth gritted in determination but still unable to succeed. The others were in equal states of incapacity and Mary stood there with her mouth open, not knowing what to do. She had seen some strange things in her career, but this was way beyond her nursing experience.

Mary took pity on this weakened and powerless coven of witches and not realising the potential consequences of her actions she decided to help. She took the bunch of keys from Emrick's pocket and opened the door to his secret cupboard.

For emergencies only! She remembered him telling her. If this wasn't an emergency then nothing was. Mary turned the key and

174

opened the door. It was stiff, and it took more than a little convincing to open, but as it did, she wished she hadn't. What she saw in the cupboard was unforgettable and quite frankly so monstrously frightening that she shut the door immediately. It was too late. What lay beyond the door let out a terrible screech that created an energy so fierce it could have easily whipped up a storm.

The force knocked Mary off her feet, catapulting her backward and straight through the open window and onto the grassy verge beyond. Winded and shocked she lay there staring at the sky above her, frozen in fear. Now she too was unable to move a muscle. With the spell wearing off, Emrick was finding his feet. He hoisted himself up from the floor, brushed himself down, clicked his knuckles and went over to his cupboard. The doors were flapping open, and a terrifying noise could be heard coming from inside, a wailing, phlegmy coughing noise, then a bang and the sound of a rattling chain.

"There, there." Emrick said softly, "I'm sorry you had no warning." He then called Charlie over who was now wandering unsteadily on his feet looking disoriented. The monstrous noise in the cupboard had now stopped and Charlie could just hear a faint purring. He stumbled toward Emrick fully expecting to see a cat inside the cupboard. He smiled. Charlie liked cats.

Charlie had seen a lot of peculiar happenings in his life, some pleasant, some not so pleasant and some downright horrific, but nothing had prepared him for what was in that cupboard. He had sensed that something wasn't quite right when he looked at Emrick; he'd seemed somewhat deranged, with his wide staring eyes and clenched jaw.

"Come on boy, I need you to help me," he said to Charlie, who now had sweat droplets, dripping from his forehead, and was wiping them with his black velvet sleeve. Despite his apprehension he did as he was instructed and went over to the cupboard. He peeked inside and a monstrous demon glared back at him. Charlie shrieked and stepped back, closing his eyes to avoid its stare. The creature hissed at him and adopted the stance of an animal about to attack. It had a metal collar around its neck, and it was chained to a large metal ring fixed to the wall. There was evidence of it having been fed, fairly recently by the looks of it, as it still had meat between its teeth and there were freshly scraped bones scattered around.

Once Charlie was sure it was chained up, he decided to bite the bullet and get closer, more out of curiosity than anything as the smell emanating from it was repugnant. The creature seemed calmer now and Charlie was able to see what it looked like. It was stood upright and was about a metre tall with a head similar to that of a domesticated cat only much bigger with little pointy horns. Its eyes were also feline but of the brightest red, and its body looked almost human, lean, and muscular, with hands and feet and huge pointed nails. It was covered from head to toe in coarse black fur and its teeth were spindly and sharp enough to easily tear the flesh from bones. The creature stared at him for a moment and then sat down, crossed legged on the floor, and proceeded to pick bits of meat from his teeth using its pointy nails.

Emrick looked at Charlie and then over to Bella who was still fiddling with her neck. He scanned the room for other survivors, but it seemed the rest of them were still frozen, unable to move or worse. Emrick had to think quickly as he knew time was of the essence. They had been preparing for this moment for some time and he knew they had to find the girl before it was too late, or their work would have been in vain. Emrick also knew that *this* spell was more powerful this time and he wasn't sure if he could break it, but he would give it a shot.

"Bella, can you talk?" Emrick asked, already knowing the answer would be no, or she would have been talking all over him by now.

"Urgh mmm, argh," was all she could muster whilst frantically pointing at her back to front head. Then she shuffled toward her broomstick and pointed at a drawstring bag that was tied to the willow twigs.

"Urgh argh urgh," she spluttered.

Emrick seemed to understand what she meant so untied the bag and took it to her. Bella grabbed it off him, took out her wand and some pouches of special powder and gestured for him and for Charlie to get their wands. Together, they managed a half decent unbinding spell. In a flash Bella's head spun back around to face the right way, then she took a sharp intake of breath and tested her vocal cords.

"ABOUT TIME YOU IMBECILE!" She screamed at Emrick and hit him around the head with her wand. "Now get Apollyon and we can go, NOW!" She screeched.

"What about me? Am I coming too?" asked Charlie, hoping he was important enough to take along.

"I suppose we could make use of you." Bella said curling her lip. Charlie grinned and looked around the room. He saw his mother laying on the floor still paralysed, a look of fear on her face, frozen in place. It made Charlie shudder. He looked at the others who were equally debilitated and he wondered if he should do something to help them, but before he could make that suggestion, he was told to be quiet and instructed to fetch Emrick's spare broomstick. Despite his keenness he was also scared to death of the pair of them, and the monster in the cupboard. *What was he called?*

"Apollyon, my darling," said Bella as she marched quickly over to the cupboard. He had obviously heard her voice before and responded with a loud purr that resounded around the room.

"We won't forget you," she added as she unleashed the beast and led him over to her broomstick. Apollyon strutted along beside her, watching Bella with admiration. She tickled him under his chin, and he flicked his tail and arched his back before getting astride her broomstick.

Charlie looked on in astonishment at her rapport with this beast, feeling a mixture of fear and envy. Wiping the sweat from his brow, he made himself comfortable on the back of Emrick's broomstick. Apollyon turned and looked Charlie in the eye and hissed at him, in a *back off she's mine* kind of way. Moments later they were flying through the night sky in the direction of the stone circle.

Bella took the lead of course, sniffing the air for even the slightest whiff of sweet apples, Apollyon holding on to her tightly, with Emrick on his broomstick and Charlie sat behind, with his arms folded inside Emrick's cape to keep warm. The wind whistled as they cut swiftly through the air and Charlie looked back at the fading lights of the hospital and thought about his mother. He felt sad leaving her there, but he decided to put his feelings aside for now. Charlie had a job to do, and he would make his

mother proud. Then, maybe, he could get a
broomstick of his own.

CHAPTER 27

The barn owl led Misty back to the edge of the forest and to the same wooden gate as before. Only this time she felt more prepared and was  comfortable with her newfound floatiness. In fact, she loved it and used her arms to soar above the trees. Misty marvelled that she could see over the treetops for miles, then she remembered why she was there and scolded herself for getting distracted. She looked down at the gate and saw the old woman stood behind it. They stared at each other for a moment, their eyes locked, and Misty's hearing intensified, like it had done before. She could hear the beating of her heart in her ears like a *Boom, Boom, Boom,* so loud it was deafening, and she felt herself start to panic so she looked at her hands to ground herself. Th old woman beckoned her, and she brought herself down to just in front of the gate. Misty looked up into the old woman's piercing green ey and a calmness came over her. Then she addressed her.

"Goddess of the Crossroads," she said, and the old woman nodded.

"Are you ready?" The old woman asked, her voice rippled like water.

"I'm ready." Misty answered.

"Then knock," the old woman said, and so Misty knocked the gate three times.

On the third knock the old woman opened the gate and stood aside for her to walk through.

"Where do I go?" She asked, and the old woman pointed with her gnarly forefinger.

"Follow the path to the wise one." Then she closed the gate and was gone.

Misty couldn't see any path. She looked at the ground which was heavily overgrown and guessed that nobody had trodden it for a very long time. However, she had told the old woman she was ready and so ready she would be. She would follow the path to the wise one.

It was dark inside the forest but just like her hearing had heightened, so too had her sight, and she was able to see even the tiniest blade of grass. The air was still thick, like soup, but she felt more normal now, less dreamy, and more like her usual self, so rather than float she decided to walk to make it easier to navigate through the forest.

As she made her way, she saw different creatures scuttling by, some even stopped to look at her. They ranged from mice and foxes to fantastical beings that she had never even seen in books and couldn't comprehend. There were also little people with big eyes peering from behind trees, and fairy beings similar to Fiona darting around, leaving trails of colours behind them. She tried to speak to them but as soon as she did they would dart away. Misty could hear mutterings and rustling, and she thought she heard them giggling and talking about her. She also heard the trees swaying and moaning and then when she listened harder, she could hear them making music. She realised it was the same tune that Wendy played on her flute. The forest was alive, and she felt a part of it. It was welcoming her in and so she kept going, further and further in until suddenly everything went quiet.

All Misty could hear now was the sound of her heart beating in her chest. She looked around and although she couldn't see any movement she knew she wasn't alone, in fact she felt there were hundreds of eyes watching her. Ahead of her she saw the biggest oak tree she had ever seen. It was as wide as a house and as tall as the tower block, she called home. Its branches were as wide as it was tall, with some of the other tree's branches intertwined; it was as if they were woven into a blanket. She stopped and knew at that moment she had arrived.

"Hello, are you the wise one?" She asked the tree.

From behind her, a barn owl flew silently over her head and came down to perch on one of the old oak's lower branches. The owl transformed into the old woman. She jumped down off the branch and stood in front of the tree and smiled.

"Meet Duir," she said and called her over.

Misty felt her body float up into the air and as she did, Duir stretched out a branch and grasped her around her waist. The tree brought her to them, then gently released its grasp allowing her to jump down onto the ground. She looked up and could see a ladder attached to Duir's trunk that stretched up as far as she could see. It was made from smaller branches and seemed to be growing out from the tree itself. Then she heard something else. It began as a low rumble which got louder until the tree started to vibrate. She noticed that all the eyes that she had thought were watching her began to appear from behind the other trees, and creatures from all around had gathered, and were now silently watching.

"Duir has given you permission to see," said the old woman to Misty. "He believes you are ready," she added and motioned for her to climb the ladder.

Misty wondered if it would be easier to float but decided not to argue and took her first step. She clung to each branch as she climbed and with each step, she felt stronger and more agile, and so she climbed up and up, until the ladder finally came to an end. Taking a deep breath, she looked down. She felt giddy and almost lost her grip as she realised how far up she had climbed. Duir was so much taller than the other trees in the forest and the view from the top was spectacular. Misty could see everything for miles around. She noticed the stone circle lit up, by the light of the fire, and she could just about make out the people sat around it. She wondered if she was still there, asleep under the blanket. Misty looked to the distance and saw the city lit up with an orange glow encircling it, she thought it looked small, and that she didn't miss it. She stretched her neck back and gazed in awe at the stars, the clouds, and the moon.

"Hello sister," she whispered.

She surveyed the world around her for what seemed like an age and wondered what it was that Duir was allowing her to see. Misty realised it wasn't just her eyes that allowed her to see, she had to see with all her senses, including her spirit. Yes, Duir was showing her a new understanding of everything, in order for it to make sense to her. She could now see that everything that was happening had a purpose, nothing was random, everything had a connection, and she was connected to everything. Satisfied with this insight she closed her eyes and when she opened them she could see white shimmering lines above her head. They were like silver cables that connected through the sky and followed the curve of the world like a giant spider's web. She stood up and stretched her arms upward as far as she could go without losing her balance,

185

trying to reach them but couldn't quite manage it.

The lines connect everything. She heard the words in her head, but they felt like they came from within the branches.

"Why are you showing me?" She asked.

You are ready, was all she heard.

As Misty pondered on being *ready,* a tremendous wind had picked up. She felt Duir swaying beneath her and heard a loud groaning noise from within the trunk. She felt the vibration from each branch as they blew in the wind, and she had to cling on tightly whilst she swung from side to side. As she held on, looking up at the shimmering lines above her head she saw what looked like two flying broomsticks, and whoever was flying them was following a line that seemed to be heading toward the stone circle. As they passed overhead, she had a terrible feeling in her gut and prickles on the back of her neck. One of the riders looked down and saw her on the treetop. Misty recognised her immediately.

"Aunt Bella," she said to herself, the riders paused for a moment, and then changed course as Misty prepared her descent.

The old woman was waiting for her when she reached the bottom. Misty noticed that she was holding a beautiful broomstick and a wand which she presented her.

"Duir has asked me to give you these. They are part of him and will serve you well."

The old woman's face was glowing white, and her voice was gentle like summer rain. Her green eyes sparkled, her dress shimmered, and she disintegrated into particles of light, before disappearing completely. Misty held the broomstick and wand, one in each hand, and they felt perfect to her. She could see the wand was skilfully fashioned from oak and the broom from oak and willow. She noticed some carved runes on each of them and wondered what they meant. She threw her arms around Duir's huge trunk and inhaled the woody smell emanating from the rough bark and whispered.

"Thank you." Misty left the forest proudly holding her broomstick and wand and when she approached the wooden gate she could see the barn owl perched on the post. It winked at her and flew away.

It's now or never, she thought straddling her broomstick, while focusing on a shimmering line above her head, she was off, flying through the sky to the stone circle.

CHAPTER 28

The stone circle was about four thousand years old, give or take, and it had always been a special place for Wendy. She could trace her ancestors back to the time of its construction and was fully aware of the stones' magical purpose. The magic wasn't just in the stones themselves, there was a web of energy lines under the ground that connected beneath the centre of the circle. This connection created a portal to other worlds which, if the conditions were right, could be accessed. She had also introduced other witches to its secrets but unfortunately there had been a few mishaps along the way.

One of those mishaps happened just forty years ago when Celeste and Bella were born to their mother Agnes, one of Wendy's most beloved witches. The birthing ceremony took place at the stones and the babies were delivered by Wendy, who like a lot of old witches was also a midwife. However, on this occasion something terrible happened. The portal opened.

Bella who was born five minutes before Celeste, had been placed in her father Peter's arms while Celeste was being delivered. However, Bella was snatched away by an entity that had come from beyond the portal. Peter saw nothing but black smoke before she disappeared. Both parents and Wendy were distraught, and Wendy vowed to get her back. Ten days later she did so and returned her immediately to her parents and sister. Only Wendy knew what had happened to Bella during her disappearance and she had never shared the details. Nor had she forgiven herself for what happened. Ever since she had wanted to rectify the tragedy, but the conditions needed to be perfect for it to be effective.

Wendy was hopeful that the conditions were now perfect. She had everyone at the stone circle that needed to be there and had given consideration that once again, some mishap may occur, but she was fairly confident that her plan was going to go the way that she intended. After all, she had been preparing for this day for forty years. She was ready.

Robert and Michael were still fast asleep and everyone else was in a deep state of concentration. There was very little noise, with just the occasional snort and snore from the sleeping pair, the hoot of an owl, and Shadow purring contently next to the fire, which was slowly burning down. Misty was also still asleep, tucked up under a blanket. Wendy was sat next to her keeping a watchful eye, ready for when she woke, and she was counting on it happening within the next few minutes as judging by the position of the moon it was getting on for one o'clock. She looked at Misty and could see her eyes were still flickering, indicating she was still in another realm, so she would have to be patient as waking her before she was ready could spoil everything.

Meanwhile, Misty was having the best time on her new broomstick. She had gotten, ever so slightly distracted, and had totally forgotten about the ceremony or her Aunt Bella. She swooped and soared through the sky, skimming the trees, and looping the loop. She felt the air blow through her fingers as she held her hand up and waved at the moon.

"Helloooooooooo sister Mooooooon." She called, and then she heard someone call her name.

Misty.

She brought her broomstick to a stop and hovered over a hill not far from the stones and listened. The night was still, with not even a breeze, but then she heard it again.

Misty, your feet, think of your feet.

A big gust of wind carried her forward with the tune of Wendy's flute whistling along with it. The smell of apple crumble followed on the wind, and then she remembered. She remembered what Wendy had told her to do to return.

"My feet," she said out loud, and looked at her feet. They were in shabby brown boots with laces. She focused on them some more and closed her eyes.

"My feet," she said again and opened her eyes.

"At last!" Wendy said as Misty opened her eyes and let out a sharp deep breath.

Misty looked around and saw she was back at the stone circle with the others. She checked to see if her mum, father, and brother were there and breathed out, relieved that she hadn't dreamt it all. Then she got up, threw the blanket off and looked around frantically.

"Are you looking for these?" Wendy asked as she showed Misty the broomstick and wand that she held in her hands. Misty took them from her and held them close, delighted that they had returned to the real world with her.

"You earned them Misty Morgan, Witch of Elphame." said Wendy, and presented her with a specially made turquoise velvet cloak and pointed hat.

"Now, put them on."

Misty did so and wearing the most beautiful clothes she had ever seen, having her own broomstick and wand given to her from the wise old oak, she felt the part.

A proper witch. But what or who is Elphame? she wondered.

Misty sat down between Wendy and her mum and tried to get comfortable but was distracted by the faint sound of ticking coming from inside her cloak. She felt around and could tell there was something heavy in there, so she rummaged around in the pockets and pulled out a handful of apple smelling feathers, a mint humbug and her mother's old pocket watch.

Wendy must have put them there, she thought.

She looked at the pocket watch and noticed the Rune markings on it matched the ones she had seen on the wooden gate. That couldn't be a coincidence surely? Misty held it in her hand and squeezed. It felt warm and the ticking was comforting. She put it back in her pocket and tried to focus on the goings on, which judging by the serious looks on everyone's faces, was extraordinarily important.

However, there was something not quite right. Misty could feel a burning sensation on the back of her neck and had the feeling she was being watched. She looked around and everyone there had their eyes closed, apart from Shadow, but he wasn't looking at her. His eyes were wide open, his pupils huge, reflecting like mirrors, and he was staring in the direction of the largest standing stone. She could see his ears twitch and his tail flick, so she guessed he could see something. Shadow noticed everything, especially if it moved quickly, and his hearing was perfect. She watched his behaviour become increasingly disturbed and she heard a low growling noise rising from his belly to his throat, and then he was gone, into the shadows and beyond the stones.

Before Misty could say anything, the silence was broken by the sound of a sharp metallic ping. It was coming from a ceremonial bell that Fiona was holding, and startled by it, Misty immediately forgot her concern for Shadow and returned her attention back to the ceremony. Fiona pinged it two more times and the Lord of the Hunt came forward.

"It is time," he said whilst standing in the centre of the circle, his hooves up on the glowing hot embers of the fire. Misty marvelled that he didn't wince or blister from the heat.

"I call upon you all to open the portal," he said, addressing the witches who were now on their feet, holding hands, with their eyes fixed on the moon that was directly above them. Misty joined them, linking her fingers with Wendy and her mother. With his arms now stretched upward and holding his wand in his right hand, the Lord of the Hunt spoke the incantation loudly.

"YE OLD GODS,
WE CALL THEE FORTH
WITH PURE HEARTS WE TREAD THE PATH
TO OPEN THE LABYRINTH WITHIN
SO AS WE DO PROTECT OUR KIN
TO BANISH DARKNESS AND RETURN TO LIGHT
WE OFFER SACRIFICE FOR OUR FLIGHT."

He stepped aside and drew a circle around the glowing embers with his wand. The circle became fire, then the flames became smoke, then mist, then droplets of water, then a pool and finally a swirling vortex remained where the fire pit once was.

Wendy stepped forward releasing her fingers from Misty's and was holding a doll in her other hand. The doll was made of white cloth that was neatly stitched together with black twine and had a faceless head with white wool for hair. It seemed to be stuffed with feathers and had the distinctive smell of apple crumble. It was dressed in a purple cloak and hat and had a W stitched on the back. Wendy handed it to Misty and looked her in the eyes.

"Look after my poppet, for if I return I want to be in one piece. Keep it hidden, keep it safe."

Without any hesitation Wendy turned and jumped into the portal. The sound of the wind whistling followed, and she was gone. Misty gasped, both shocked and horrified at what had just happened. She sat holding the poppet doll in her hands wondering what, if anything, she should do. She looked around to judge the situation, but nobody else looked troubled that Wendy had jumped into a swirling hole of nothingness and by the look on their faces they actually seemed pleased, Misty however, was confused.

Shadow ran past at the speed of light being chased by something quite absurd. It looked like another cat but much larger and running on its hind legs; its eyes glowed red and it smelled of rotten meat. The portal was still open. The witches watched as Shadow jumped through followed by the foul-smelling creature, and they too were gone, swallowed up by the swirling vortex into the world beyond. A loud scream could be heard from above, and the witches looked up to see Bella on her broomstick hovering over them.

"Apollyon. No!" Bella screamed. But before she could do anything the Lord of the Hunt closed the portal with his sword, using it in the same way as a key locking a door.

"AS ABOVE SO BELOW,
SO, MOTE IT BE."

His loud voice boomed.

A flash of light emanated from the portal and then there was darkness. The vortex was gone, and the portal was closed, it was as if it had never been there at all. The blood-curdling scream echoing out from Bella was so loud that it seemed to shake the ground. Bella and Emrick, with Charlie still on the back, hovered above the circle. They knew they were unable to land due to the protection of the circle. So, instead, they stared menacingly at the group of witches, with little to no effect. Misty ignored them, as did the others. She hadn't even realised that Charlie was there, and she didn't care. She just sat there staring at the poppet that Wendy had given her, feeling overcome with sadness. Wendy had only just gone and yet Misty missed her already, she felt as though she had lost a part of her, and Shadow too. It felt too awful for words. Misty held the poppet in her hands staring at its strange faceless head. She knew it was meant to represent Wendy and held it close to her heart. Misty wished she was with her, tears welled in her eyes and although she tried to force them back, one splashed on the poppet's face causing it to blemish as she wiped it. Then she remembered Wendy's last words to her, so she tucked it into her cloak pocket, to keep it hidden, to keep it safe.

Misty looked around and saw the other witches getting themselves ready to leave, muttering to each other, hugging, and smiling. She saw Eli had transformed back to his usual self and noticed he too was smiling. Her father and Michael were sitting up yawning and wondering what they just missed. Celeste saw that Misty looked upset and went over to her.

"Why is everyone so happy? Wendy and Shadow are gone. I don't get it," said Misty with tears falling down her cheeks.

Celeste held her chin and looked into her eyes.

"It's not over Misty, it's just beginning."
Then they both heard something and looked
up. There was Bella, Emrick, and Charlie
hovering on their broomsticks above them
laughing. In a split second they were gone,
flying the white lines that Misty could now see
quite clearly. Sadly, Misty got up and still
holding her broomstick and wand headed back
to the bus with the others.

CHAPTER 29

The witches packed up their things, loaded the bus and made sure there was no litter or damage from their time at the stone circle.

"It must be left as we found it," explained Eli.

Misty clambered onto the bus, still holding on to her broomstick and wand, her poppet safely hidden away in her new turquoise cloak. She looked around at all the happy faces and struggled to understand it.

"Nobody seems bothered about Wendy." She said loudly, "she could be trapped or in danger, surely we need to help her?"

She looked at her mum hoping she would say something reassuring.

"Wendy chose to go my darling, I know it's hard to understand right now but she had been preparing for that moment for many years, you will understand in time," she said as she put her arm around Misty's shoulder and snuggled into her.

"I'll miss her, that's all." Misty said.

"Me too Misty, me too," said Celeste and they both turned to look out of the window.

It was still very dark outside, and they could only see their own reflections in the window, but Misty could have sworn she saw Wendy's face looking at her.

Impossible, she thought, and closed her eyes. When she opened them, Wendy was gone.

Michael and Robert sat together in silence with neither knowing what to say to each other. Despite the fact, that they'd been asleep throughout the ceremony, they both felt exhausted, like they'd been busy doing something but didn't know what. They sat there, thinking, processing, recapping, and essentially trying to make sense of it all but not really getting anywhere. Celeste however snuggled up to her daughter, content that the family were back together at last.

The bus journey back to the city was quiet and uneventful. The witches had been expecting retaliation so had placed a protection spell around the bus and had other spells up their sleeves to use if need be. However, they needn't have concerned themselves, as Bella, Emrick, and Charlie were flying back to the hospital. They had no intention of causing any mayhem, at least not tonight. They had instead decided to regroup and figure out their revenge.

Rudy dropped everyone off one by one and each of them said their farewells. Misty, who was still upset said nothing. She could see their stop was approaching, and her stomach knotted. She looked at her father and saw him getting his shoes back on and fumbling on the floor for his coat. Misty nudged her mum.

"Are you and Michael going to live with us now?" She asked hopefully, "I know there's not much room but ..."

Celeste interrupted. "Misty, Michael, Robert. How do we feel about going back home? I mean *our* home," she smiled.

"Seriously?" Michael asked.

"Can we go there now?" Asked Misty, her stomach knots flipped and did a somersault.

This was something she'd been dreaming of but never thought it would happen.

"It's decided then. Robert, I hope you remember where you hid the key?" Celeste said to her husband. He nodded.

"I'd never forget," he said with a smile. So, with a short detour, Rudy's bus was back on the motorway and heading south, to their secluded old cottage on the edge of the woods. Back to their home.

The journey took them down quiet roads and country lanes. The bus was too big to get down the final dirt track, so Rudy parked the bus up and helped guide their way with his flashlight down the overgrown path until they reached the old iron gate. Despite the offer of staying the night Rudy politely declined. He was tired and longed to be tucked up in his own bed with a hot cocoa, so he headed back to the city.

With Rudy gone, the realisation of being home as a family began to dawn on them. It had been five long years since they had been there, and the surrounding wall and iron gate was now covered in ivy and brambles and the padlock rusty. Robert, just using the light from his phone, wandered off in the direction of the giant oak tree called Jack, and returned with a grin jangling a set of old rusty keys.

"Safe and sound, thanks to *Old Jack*," and with a bit of elbow grease the lock sprung open.

The front door opened with a creak, and they all peered hopefully through the doorway. Misty coughed. It was dark, dusty, and smelled of damp. Her heart sank as it wasn't at all as she remembered it. She could hear scratching noises and the squeaking of mice, there were cobwebs hanging down and the thought of spiders crawling on her made her shudder. At that moment she felt like turning around and going back to the city; at least the grotty flat was warm and familiar. Despite his initial hesitation Robert went in first. He wiped the cobwebs he could reach from the ceiling and found the light switch. The light, rather than making it more inviting, had the opposite effect and highlighted the awful state the abandoned home was in, but Robert tried his very best to be positive.

"A deep clean and a lick of paint and it will be just as we remember it, come on guys we are home at last."

They all agreed that to be together, back in their own home was indeed the best thing to happen in years and so they decided as a family that they would make it work, starting now. They spent the rest of that night on the big orange sofa, cuddled up for warmth and slept deeply and soundly. They were woken in the morning by a loud *cock-a-doodle-do* at the window.

"Jeffrey?" Misty jumped up and ran out into the garden.

It can't be? She looked around. The garden was totally overgrown with weeds and nettles, but it was otherwise the beautiful oasis she remembered. Some of the chickens had survived too, with Jeffrey the cockerel happily pecking away in the undergrowth. He looked up and stared at her for a few moments and then carried on pecking.

The sun was coming up now and the golden flecks of light bounced off the evergreen shrubs and peeked through the gaps of the almost bare trees. Misty closed her eyes and breathed in the garden. It smelled so different from the city. It also sounded different, and she felt different as well. She felt free, she felt safe, and she didn't want to go back to the city ever again

Now where is Jack? she wondered, as she searched the garden. Misty guessed the garden was about the size of a football pitch and it had many different types of trees within the surrounding stone walls, which made it difficult to locate this one particular tree. She spent quite some time trudging through the long grass, trampling the nettles, looking intently for her very own Duir. She had a strong urge to find the old oak, especially now she knew that Wendy had planted him. It gave her comfort knowing that she had lived on the same land, in the same woods all those years ago; she somehow felt closer to her.

Misty found him quite easily in the end and couldn't understand how she could have forgotten where he was. She threw her arms around his huge trunk and kissed him, then held her ear close to his rough bark and heard a boom, boom, boom, which could have been the pulse of her own heart. She wasn't sure.

"Misty!" she heard her mum calling her, so she ran back inside. "We need to go back to the flat to get your dad's car and your things. We've got a cab waiting, do you want to come?" Celeste asked.

Misty really didn't want to go back, not even for a moment and now that she had found her old friend she decided to stay put.

"No, it's ok, I'll see you later." Misty shouted, already heading back to the garden.

Still dressed in her cloak and pointed hat, Misty climbed her old oak friend Jack, not too far up but just to the first big branch that was comfortable enough to sit on. It was five years since she last sat there. Being just seven years old she hadn't really understood what was happening at the time and just remembered sitting on the branch and crying.

The memories were vague, but the feelings were still strong, and she had a flash of seeing her mother being taken away, her father being angry and shouting at her and seeing her brother screaming. Then she had another flash, it was Aunt Bella, she was there too. These were not memories she wished to dwell on and for the past five years had put those images in a box within her mind and closed the lid. Now sat on the branch the lid had opened just a little. That scared her, so she shut the lid tight again.

Still sat on the branch she rummaged in her pocket and brought out the poppet. She sniffed it and imagined Wendy's face, her eyes, her smile, and her funny little mannerisms. She wondered what she was doing and remembered that Wendy had told her to look after the poppet to keep her safe, so that is what she would do. She started to climb down Old Jack and noticed a box nailed to the side of the trunk, partially hidden by some ivy. She saw that it had a door which was slightly open. Intrigued, she looked inside but it was empty.

Fathers secret key box! She thought, *what a great place to keep the poppet safe, and hidden.*

Misty placed the poppet inside and shut the door firmly.

"Look after her, Jack." She said to the old oak and clambered down.

The day passed quickly and when her parents and Michael returned, Misty helped them with the few belongings they'd managed to fit in the car. She was pleased to see that they had squeezed the old grandfather clock in, and even more pleased that they had remembered Mum's box of magical items, which also contained her Book of Shadows. She spent the rest of the day arranging her bedroom while her parents cleaned, washed clothes, and did all the other things necessary for them to feel comfortable. They even watched some TV and Robert set up the WIFI. Things felt unusually normal for a change and the family needed that.

As Misty sat on her newly laundered bed, she looked out of her window and saw Old Jack. She watched as the wind blew through his branches and he shed the last of his leaves. She thought of the poppet in the box and hoped she was still safe and sound. Then her thoughts were interrupted by a delicious smell coming from the kitchen. She smiled, jumped up and ran downstairs in time to see her mum bring a piping hot, still bubbling apple crumble out of the oven. Celeste looked at her knowingly.

"I think we deserve something nice," she said, "to remember Wendy."

That night they all went to bed with a full belly and a room to call their own. Misty placed her special items away in a cupboard, leaving just her wand and her Book of Shadows by her bed just in case. Given recent events, she wanted to be prepared for anything.

"Good night Wendy and good night Shadow, wherever you are," she whispered, and closed her eyes. The wind gently rattled the window, as if it were saying *"goodnight"* back to her.

CHAPTER 30

That night Misty had a dream that she was flying on her broomstick with Wendy and Shadow flying next to her. The air was chilly, and the sun was just coming up over the horizon. She could smell the scent of sweet apples wafting around her as they looped, dive bombed, and raced through the clouds. They paused to hover over a group of crows' nests and watched the hatchlings open their beaks expectantly. She could hear the cawing of the mother crow as she eyed them from a nearby tree. Finally, they waved goodbye to each other, even Shadow raised his paw and then they were gone, over the treetops and out of sight. The dream was typically fragile with the images evaporating like steam from a kettle, and when she woke in the morning they had almost gone completely. All that remained was a strong feeling that something wonderful had happened during the night.

Misty lay in her bed with the duvet wrapped snuggly around her with just her head poking out. She was still adjusting to being back in her old bedroom. It felt strange to be back there, but she also felt quite safe. She lay there staring at the ceiling, watching the cobwebs blowing lightly from a draft in the old window. While watching them blowing back and forth, her thoughts drifted back to her time with Duir, and now having been reacquainted with Old Jack she wondered if she could make herself come out of her body, like in her dreams. She decided to give it a go.

Misty continued to focus on the draughty cobwebs, watching them blowing back and forth, back, and forth, over, and over until her eyes felt heavy. Then she focused on feeling her feet, then her legs and then her hands. She noticed she had already started to feel lighter, so she focused next on her tummy, then her chest and then her head.

Oooh! I feel odd, she thought, as she noticed her breathing was getting slower and deeper. She imagined herself separating, moving away from herself and then she felt a tickling sensation in her bellybutton, followed by a booming noise. Then it happened, she was out. She floated out of herself and looked down at her other self still wide awake on the bed. The space between them was soupy, wavy, and thick, but she could clearly see herself. Misty smiled at herself, in fact they both smiled at each other. She wasn't sure which one of herself was doing what, and so she decided she must be doing both.

How peculiar, she thought, but not half as peculiar as everything else that had happened recently, so she wasn't scared.

Misty was very excited that she had been able to do this herself. She remembered the other witches had told her they could *walk between the worlds,* and she wondered if this was what they meant. She waved goodbye to herself still laying on the bed and floated out through the window. She found her way to Old Jack and sat on the same branch as the day before. Old Jack groaned and she held her ear close to his rough bark. She could just about make out some words, which sounded like *time* and *Wendy,* then his groaning grew louder, and he started to sway. Misty held on tightly as a wind, almost like a whirlwind, came upon them. The wind whistled the familiar tune of Wendy's flute. Misty hummed along whilst she watched the swirling air and branches sweep around her, then the wind stopped. She suddenly knew what she had to do. It was as if Old Jack was telling her. She got out her pocket watch that was still in her cloak, and her wand, and she noticed they felt solid and not at all dreamlike. She touched the watch with her wand and spoke an incantation, the words flowing from her mouth without any thought.

"Remove the chains of space and time
To when we were around
When old Jack was an acorn small
And planted in this ground."

Misty watched as the pocket watch hands went backwards at an incredible speed. She was unable to count the times they went around the numbers, but she would guess at hundreds. Then it stopped. Misty felt dizzy. She felt as though she was falling and everything around her was foggy. She felt around with her hands and could tell she was no longer in the tree but sat on the grass. It was damp, and there was an earthy smell, like freshly dug soil. Then she felt a gust of wind blow around her, and the faint smell of apples was wafting along with it. She felt someone gently tap her shoulder three times.

Misty turned to look and as she did the wind stopped and the fog cleared, and there before her was a young woman of about twenty years old. She had a kind face and reminded her of Wendy, but it couldn't be. She had dark brown hair, which was curled into spirals beneath a purple bonnet, and she wore a purple dress revealing white petticoats beneath. She had a white crocheted apron and a shawl around her shoulders, her feet were bare, and she was holding a wicker basket.

"Wendy?" Misty asked her tentatively, "Is that you?" The young woman laughed.

"My oh my, here you are! I am Gwendolyn, but you can call me Wendy if you like?"

Misty's jaw fell open in shock, her spell had worked. "Oh yes, but you don't know me yet," she said.

"Ha-ha. Oh, yes I do, you are the Witch of Elphame, but you're known as Misty." Wendy said.

For the next few hours, the two of them chatted and spoke about things that had happened and things to come. Wendy showed her around the garden and the house. It was quite different from how it was in Misty's time, but she could tell it was the same land. The wood just looked thicker and the now dilapidated stone wall was newly built and perfect. As they both stood admiring the perfectly tended garden, which was filled with magical plants and herbs, Misty felt something rub against her legs. She looked down to see a cat, a black and white cat with big yellow sparkly eyes, who was now rubbing the side of his mouth against her legs.

"Meet Merlin." Wendy said as she scooped him up into her arms and held him like a baby. She kissed his nose and then put him down. He flopped by her feet and rolled on his back allowing Misty to tickle him.

"Is he just a cat?" She asked. Wendy looked at her with interest.

"Of course, he is. What did you think he was?" And they both laughed together, Misty now feeling a bit silly. "He is very special though." Wendy added with a wink.

Misty sat on the damp grass with Merlin snuggling into her, whilst Wendy went into the house. She returned holding an acorn, which had already started to sprout. Misty shrieked with delight as she held out her hand to show her.

"Old Jack!" she cried. Wendy smiled.

"I dreamt that this would be the day I would meet you and we would plant the acorn," she said, "Now we shall name him Young Jack."

Misty grinned from ear to ear and nodded vigorously. They made a hole in the ground and planted it together. Whilst doing so they sang a rhyme, repeating it nine times with Misty following Wendy's lead.

"Power of the Oak
Mighty Jack we invoke
From acorn and root Wassail
To branch and leaf, all hail."

When they finished, they watered Young Jack, then hand in hand they circled the spot nine times.

"Now it's time for celebrating," said Wendy and she went inside for her flute. She played the tune that Misty was now so familiar with, and they danced together around the site of the planted acorn.

When Wendy stopped playing, she went inside again and came out with a tray, balancing two cups of apple juice and two bowls of stewed apple with crunchy cake topping.

"Help yourself Misty, I made it specially." Wendy said. "The apples are from the tree over there."

Wendy pointed at a big tree which had already shed its leaves, but still had a few old apples on the upper branches. Misty ate it heartily, it tasted so good.

Just like Mum's, she thought, and the juice was sweet like nectar. Satisfied she flopped to the ground and Merlin came over to her and sniffed her face.

"We will meet again." Misty heard him speak inside her head. She sat up and looked him in the eyes. "I might look different, but it'll be me," he said without moving his mouth.

"I know you as Shadow." Misty said to him, and Merlin gave a soft meow and proceeded to wash his face with his paw. She looked up to tell Wendy, who shushed her with a finger over her lips.

"Now Misty, it's nearly time for you to return, your magic can only be sustained for a short while so it's important that I share one more detail with you." Wendy had a serious look in her eyes which made Misty sit up straight. "As you know we will meet again in more than four hundred years' time. What happens from now mustn't affect the time between, so when we do meet again you will not remember that we have had this time together.

But be sure a part of you will know. Now when you go home you must learn your shape, mine is crow, yours might be too, it is for you to discover."

Misty nodded, she already felt crow so that would be simple she thought.

"Oh, and one more thing," said Wendy, "Don't go into the portal, just look after the poppet you told me about."

Misty nodded.

"But Wendy, what about Bella?" she asked.

"You need to go now, I can see your shine is fading," said Wendy taking the empty dish from Misty's hand. "Now go."

They said their goodbyes and Misty reluctantly prepared to be separated from Wendy for a second time. Misty took out her pocket watch and tapped it with her wand and uttered the following incantation.

"Remove the chains of space and time
For now, we do foretell
That Old Jack is now a grand oak tree
And the past we bid farewell."

The watch hands sped forward at such a speed that she was unable to count, only stopping when Misty was back in her bed. She sat up and gasped for breath. She wasn't sure how long she'd been gone but her watch indicated that it had only been a few minutes and not the several hours that it felt like. She felt exhausted and exhilarated by her adventure and never wanted to forget it, so she got out her Book of Shadows and wrote it all down, including the incantations. Misty had no idea how she was able to come up with them, and she wondered what else she would be able to do now that she was a proper witch.

I forgot to ask her about Elphame. She sighed. *Maybe Mum will know*, she wondered, and went downstairs for breakfast.

CHAPTER 31

Over the next few months Misty and her family settled into life in the country. They had restored the house back to its  former glory, and now it was Spring they were spending more time outside, especially their garden. They had all flourished in this new environment, but Robert especially was a different man. He hadn't picked up a drink for months, instead he had found a new job that paid well, and he was learning carpentry. His first project was building a new chicken coop as they had rescued six scraggy battery hens. Jeffrey particularly enjoyed the company of the new hens. He would strut around, circling and fluttering his wings attempting to get their attention. It wasn't long before the hens grew fat and sprouted beautiful new feathers, and one by one the happy hens laid delicious eggs, which Misty would collect each morning for breakfast.

It was generally accepted that the garden was Celeste's domain. She had started seeding magical and medicinal herbs ready for planting in the garden. She was quite proud of her *'witchy garden,'* as she liked to refer to it.

Although it had been unattended for five long years, some of the original plants had survived and were flourishing amidst the overgrown nettles and brambles. It didn't take Celeste long to tend and clear it in preparation for the new seedlings, and she spent many hours in the greenhouse dancing and singing whilst she worked.

Celeste had always hoped that her children would share her love of nature and she wasn't disappointed. Michael loved animals and had a special affinity with horses. He had found himself a part time job at a riding school and although he wasn't keen on mucking out the stables, he was able to ride the horses, which he did during whatever spare time he had. He would often be seen running free over the nearby hills and fields on his favourite mare Rhiannon. But it was Misty who had the green fingers. She had shown a real interest in learning about plants, especially their magical and medicinal properties, partly because she wanted to make her own potions and lotions, but also for spells. And so, Celeste and Misty were often in the garden practicing their *hedge witchery,* but what they loved the most was being together and how the bond between them was strengthening.

The relationship between Misty and Old Jack was also getting stronger. When she climbed him, she felt close to Wendy and regularly checked on the poppet which was still safely hidden in the box. Sometimes when she was quiet, she could hear noises come from inside it. The beating of a heart and whistling of the the wind were most common, but occasionally she heard the flute playing that same familiar tune, and once she even thought, she heard purring. These noises, she knew, indicated that Wendy and Shadow were alive, somewhere.

Misty's magical abilities were also improving. She was now adept at spell casting and could also bend time if the conditions were right. However, she found it drained her energy so decided she would only do so if it was absolutely necessary. She also set aside one evening a week to practice on her broomstick. She chose her timings carefully, usually at dusk and was mindful not to fly too close to any regular folk who may die of fright at the sight of a real witch!

Misty had started a new school which was in the local village. She had made a few friends but was still feeling a little unsure of who she could trust so she hadn't shared many details of her life yet; she kept the magical side private. However, the friendships within her coven were strong and they would meet up at the stone circle each month during the full moon for a special ceremony. They would always talk about Wendy and danced and sung in her honour. She never told the others, but Misty would take the poppet along with her, keeping it safe in her cape, in the hope that Wendy would know and come back to them. So far, she had heard nothing from her.

At night, just before she went to sleep, Misty would practice coming out of her body. She found that it was becoming second nature now and she could take herself out at will. However, she was only able to go so far, as fear would always bring her back. She would usually find herself travelling out into the garden and mostly spent time with Old Jack. She also had glimpses of the nature spirits that lived in the garden. She would see pixies, fairies, gnomes, and other mystical beings flitting around. They would tease her by almost showing themselves and then darting away giggling and muttering to each other. Her experiences were always quite similar and although she found them exciting, she felt there was more to see and learn. Even more importantly, there were places she needed to go, if only she wasn't so scared. Misty would often find herself seeing Aunt Bella's face watching her from beyond the wall, but would resist going any further, fearing she wasn't yet strong enough to handle whatever was out there. She also hadn't got around to asking her mum about Elphame either, so one day in March she decided to do just that.

It was a sunny day and Misty, and Celeste were in the greenhouse planting out some seedlings. Misty decided that today was as good a day as any.

"I have a question," she said as she carried on with the potting. "I've been told that I am the Witch of Elphame, but Mum, I haven't a clue what that means."

Celeste stopped what she was doing and stared at her daughter.

"Who told you this?" she asked with a sharpness that surprised Misty. "Sorry darling, you needn't answer that, it's just quite unexpected that's all." Celeste paused, as she thought of how to respond. "I'll make us some tea and we'll talk," she said, heading inside.

Celeste came back carrying a tray of tea, biscuits, and a book. Misty couldn't help but feel that her mum was a little anxious as her hands were trembling. Celeste poured the tea and handed it to Misty. Then she picked up the book.

Misty's heart skipped a beat when she recognised the book in her hand. It was leather and had Runes on the front.

Mum's Book of Shadows. She could see that it had been mended with tape from when she had broken it all those years ago but was otherwise it was in good order.

Celeste opened her Book of Shadows and flicked through, until she found the page she was looking for, she looked up at Misty.

"I had a vision when you were born," she explained. "I wrote it down in here. Let me read it to you ... On the day she was born I looked at my baby girl and I saw Runes appear on her forehead. I had no idea what they meant so I researched them and discovered that they spelled *ELPHAME*. This name means *'the bridge between the two worlds.'* She will be skilled in walking the bridge between the physical and the multi-dimensional worlds. She will be the Shining One."

Celeste closed her Book of Shadows and smiled at Misty.

"Go and get your book," she said, and Misty ran into the house and quickly came back holding it in her hands. "Let me see it." Celeste asked, and so Misty handed it to her. "You see, the Runes on the cover?" She said pointing at them. "They are the same as those at your birth, they spell out *ELPHAME!*"

Misty didn't know what to say and she still didn't really understand what it meant but she didn't want to upset her mum either.

"Is it because I can travel out of my body?" Was all she could come up with, as she looked for her mum's reaction.

"My darling, you have no idea of the power you have, but yes that is part of it." Celeste said still smiling.

That evening, Misty went to bed with her mind clearer. She thought that if she had the power of Elphame she could certainly find Wendy and Shadow. She didn't feel like travelling tonight, she was exhausted and just wanted to sleep. However, as she drifted off, she heard something that jolted her awake. A voice cackling manically came out of the darkness.

"The shining one, the Elphame, the saviour, the DEAD one."

Misty sat up, her sheets wet with sweat and her heart pounding. She recognised that voice.

"Aunt Bella!" Misty shouted.

Her Aunt's voice sounded close, so she wondered if she were in the room with her. Misty looked around in the dim light and saw the outlines of her clothes hanging on hooks.

Nothing there but clothes, she told herself. Then there was a tapping on the window, the curtains fluttered, and she could see shadows moving around outside. Misty picked up her wand and counted to three in her head before pulling back the curtain. With her wand, in her hand and ready to strike, she saw three figures silhouetted against the moonlit sky, hovering on broomsticks just beyond the far wall. Misty was frozen to the spot with fear, staring at them for what seemed an age and then in a flash they were gone.

Misty sat on her bed trying to catch her breath. Then she jumped up and went to knock on her parents' bedroom door.

"Mum! Dad!" she called, "You need to come, right NOW!"

She knew that Aunt Bella was one of the figures and she guessed another was Charlie.

She didn't know the third, it looked like a man, but she didn't know him. She lay back down on her bed clutching her wand to her chest as she waited for her parents to appear at her door. Misty could smell Duir's wooden handle, and it helped calm her a little, but the reality was now hitting home.

Aunt Bella had found them.

CHAPTER 32

The next day Misty didn't really want to discuss what she had seen outside the window, and pretended she was fine, but she knew that her worried face gave everything away. Celeste had already been on the phone  with Eli to plan an emergency coven meeting. Although she was also worried, she was also confident that they would come up with a plan and tried to reassure Misty as best she could.

"Scrambled eggs?" Robert asked as he plated up the breakfast. "Doreen laid some whoppers this morning," he added, trying to lighten the mood.

"I'm not hungry." Misty replied sullenly and went straight out into the garden.

Robert looked at Celeste and raised his eyebrows. "Should we be doing anything? I mean, what can I do to help?" He asked.

"You look after Michael and leave this to me." Celeste said with a smile. Then she kissed him on the cheek and followed Misty out into the garden.

Robert watched from the window and knew that if anyone could do anything about this situation, it was Celeste.

Celeste went straight to Old Jack as she knew that she'd find Misty there. She was right. Misty was sat on her favourite branch staring at the sky. Celeste waited for Misty to notice her before climbing up to join her. They sat together on the branch and Misty took her mother's hand and squeezed.

"I know everything will be alright. I just get scared sometimes." Misty said, looking up at her mother's face. She looked serene and reminded her of an angel.

"We all get scared Misty. But we can use our fear to get things done. The fierce energy that burns within us can transform into the most powerful magic. You must believe in yourself." Celeste said smiling. Then she pointed to the sky as a large green moth fluttered past. "I'm going to go now. I will see you later." At that, Celeste transformed into a crow and following the moth, she flew over the garden wall and disappeared from view.

Misty had never seen her mother transform before and was impressed by how effortless she made it seem. Even with her improved skills, she still hadn't found her true shape, and this bothered her immensely. She wanted so much to join the other witches in their intimate show of togetherness, as that is what it seemed to her when she saw them transforming in and out of crow form. The other witches had given her advice on what they thought could help her change, including spending time with the resident crows from the surrounding countryside. However other than making a few crow friends nothing happened. In fact, the more she tried, the more frustrated she became and often felt like giving up entirely.

Maybe I'm not meant to be a crow. Maybe I'm meant to be different? She wondered.

Feeling quietly confident in her mother's abilities to sort things out, Misty decided to distract herself with a walk. The weather was perfect and so she decided to take a picnic and explore the land further afield. She borrowed a small rucksack from Michael, made herself a peanut butter sandwich, took a chocolate mini roll from her secret stash, grabbed a carton of orange juice and off she went. She passed a crow who cawed at her from the top of a sycamore tree. She greeted it with a salute and a *"caw, caw,"* trying her best not to dwell on her failure to become one of them.

She must have only been walking for about twenty minutes when she came to a wooden gate. It wasn't dissimilar to the one near to the stone circle and having never seen it before she decided to investigate. The gate opened into a wooded area that had a well-trodden path. The trees were a mixture of oaks, ash and hawthorn which were just starting to bud. Misty followed the path until she found a clearing, and another wooden gate that opened onto a field. She could see what looked like a huge standing stone in the middle of the field and decided to head toward it. The stone was twice her height and as wide as a door and stood vertically in the ground and covered in moss and lichen. Seeing it gave her a funny feeling in her tummy and for a moment she felt like she'd seen it before but had no idea why. She smoothed it gently with her hands and in doing so it made them tingle, and a rush of excitement filled her body and her heart fluttered. Suddenly she had a vision in her mind's eye, like a flash of a memory, but she knew it couldn't be that, as she'd never been there before. She saw people dressed in white robes. She couldn't see their faces as they had hoods covering them, but she could see that they were gathering around the stone and offering it loaves of bread and fruit. Then one of the people took down their hood and looked up. Misty caught their eyes and her heart raced as she saw who it was; it was her own face staring back at her. She cried out and then the tingling stopped as suddenly as it came, and the vision was gone.

Despite trying to shake off the funny feeling it stayed with her, and although she still wasn't hungry, she decided to have her picnic to distract herself. She found a sunny spot not too far away from the standing stone and made herself comfortable. She got out her sandwich and took a bite and as she did, she noticed she was being watched by some rabbits. There were about three or four of them sat in a row in front of the standing stone. She thought they may be hungry so broke off a piece of bread and threw it in their direction, but they didn't move and just sat there staring at her.

Misty thought it most peculiar to be stared at by such nervous animals and so she stayed deadly quiet and still and watched them until they eventually hopped away. She finished her picnic and looked to see if she could see them again. She smiled to herself when she noticed they hadn't gone far and were running around together at the brow of the hill. She walked closer so she could see more clearly and realised they weren't rabbits at all, they were hares. She knew this as Michael had made a point of telling her the difference and she remembered being surprised that they were a different species altogether.

She thought the speed and grace of the hares was effortless and they looked so beautiful with their long ears pointing to the sky. She silently watched and marvelled at them until the sun went down and the moon appeared, full and large. With no light pollution from the city the hares went wild, dancing and frolicking. Misty watched, entranced and unable to contain her excitement any longer she broke her cover to join them.

The hares frolicked and danced together in the moonlight and when Misty looked above her she could see the white shimmering lines that connected everything around the earth. They ran and chased each other until she was led back to the standing stone. Together, they circled it and then stopped. Misty felt strange, something was different. She looked at her hands but instead she had furry paws. She wiggled them and then knew for sure that they belonged to her. It was at that moment she knew she had transformed. She twitched her nose and could smell the strong scent of the grass. Her new whiskers picked up vibrations from the ground and her legs enabled her to bounce high into the air, as though she was on springs. Her hearing and sense of smell were heightened, and she had the urge to eat the bark and buds from the trees. More incredible was her ability to understand what the other hares were saying to her. It was as though they could read each other's minds, and with a special twitch of the ear, she knew they were going to gather together, and that something important was going to happen.

The dew was settling on the long grass and Misty's fur glistened in the moonlight. She scratched her ears with her hind paw and yawned. One of the hares snuggled close to her and asked if she would like to join him to gaze at the moon. She thanked the hare with a tail wiggle and although she had no idea what gazing at the moon meant, she agreed and went with him.

They joined the other hares who were sat together atop of a small hill and with their heads fixed toward the sky, their eyes fixed directly on the moon above them. Although, she did not understand the reason for their action, she had a feeling they were waiting for something, and it turned out that she was right. She felt the ground tremble beneath her and then a gap appeared from within the air. Flecks of light shimmered and sparkled, and a ball of white light emerged. The ball of light fluttered above them and then it approached each hare individually. It whispered something in their ears and then moved on to the next. The other hares watched as the ball of light floated to Misty. She trembled as it spun many webs of light around her until finally, it transformed into a beautiful woman that was bathed in a shimmering white glow. Misty recognised her immediately. The Moon Goddess smiled knowingly at her, leant forward, and whispered in her long furry ears.

"You are now transformed. You are Elphame."

Misty was transfixed by her beauty and longed to gaze at her for ever, but within that moment she knew this wasn't the end. Something within her knew she would meet her again, and then she was gone. She looked around and she was alone, the moon had already moved out of sight behind the trees ready for the suns return. She could already see the orange splendour peeking over the horizon.

The hares had left Misty to go and feed in the woodland. She sat on her hind legs staring at the standing stone trying to gather her thoughts. She had started to worry about transforming back, as although she was enjoying being a hare she did enjoy being a girl too. As she wondered what to do next, she heard Wendy's voice in her head.

"Think of your feet."

YES, she thought, *that's what I must do.*

She looked at her hind paws and wiggled her furry toes, then she imagined her feet with her soft pink skin and nails. She closed her eyes and stood up. She could feel herself getting taller, rising up from the ground, and when she opened her eyes she was back to being a girl again. She breathed a sigh of relief and shook her body to make sure, a few strands of fur fell onto her shoe, and she smiled to herself remembering the black feathers that the other witches had shaken off.

Yes, she thought, she had done it at last. Satisfied she grabbed her rucksack and headed home, hoping that her parents hadn't been too worried by her disappearance.

On her way down the path to her house, a crow cawed at her and flew into the garden. Misty smiled to herself as she realised that her mum had been keeping an eye on her all along. When she entered the house, Celeste was sat in an armchair in the living room with black feathers surrounding her feet. She peered over her glasses when Misty walked through the door and smiled.

"Mum I did it!" Misty said excitedly. Celeste raised her eyebrows and smiled knowingly.

"Yes, my darling, you did." she replied.

"What happens next Mum?" Misty asked solemnly.

"Well Misty Morgan, Witch of Elphame, *that* is entirely up to you."